Praise for *The Reluctant Psychic*

~ Review 1 ~

I've just finished *The Reluctant Psychic* by Bryon Williams and thoroughly enjoyed it.

Bryon's latest offering relates the efforts of a deceased Police Detective – yes, a ghost! – to solve her own murder and a few other related crimes with the assistance of an eccentric psychic who has become disillusioned by her treatment from the police in a previous attempt to assist them with an investigation – hence 'reluctant'.

It gives an intriguing and humorous twist to the crime genre, and although the ghostly intervention might be seen as a tad 'woo-woo' by some, several TV documentaries have been made displaying both the successes and failures of psychics in searching for missing people. Given the current popularity of Sci-Fi and Fantasy on TV and in Film, and the success of shows like *Medium* and Ghost *Whisperer*, Bryon's book is a no-brainer to be adapted for television! I think there would be a huge audience out there that would love it!

~ Review 2 ~

Barbara Ramsay, South Melbourne, Victoria

Wonderful! *The Reluctant Psychic*, by Bryon Williams, is a fantastic combination of that 'other world' that we are all so fascinated with and a real 'good guys, bad guys' crime story.

The heroine is dead... that's right, she's dead, and we find that out when she dies, early in the story. She suddenly finds herself on another plane, no longer in a body...well, not an earthly one anyway.

She is now a spirit, a bodiless soul, a truly spiritual being ... but far from being a 'holier than thou', platitude-scattering do-gooder, this heroine is a feisty, clever woman… sorry… a feisty, clever *ghost*, who would be great to meet and fun to spend time with, in a body or out of one.

Her adventure takes place both on another plane and in this world, as she finds a very much alive and equally feisty psychic to help her solve an important crime… her own death! This is a psychic who is completely fed up with trying to help the police, who mocked her and treated her 'visions' with disdain. Now she is absolutely unwilling to get involved in anything, other than nice 'readings' for ordinary people, who want to get in touch with the departed.

This is a crime story with a real difference. It's funny and intriguing and surprising and it will appeal to anyone who is interested in the supernatural, enjoys the unique and loves a good crime story.

If this book became a television series, I wouldn't be a bit surprised. And I'd watch every episode!

The Reluctant Psychic

By
Bryon Williams

The Reluctant Psychic

Email: bryonwilliams@tpg.com.au

ISBN – 978-0-6484238-3-6
ISBN -

Subject: Murder mystery

Copyright Cover Design – Bryon Williams and Emma Gloede

Dedication

To my dear friend, Berrie Cameron-Allen,
for her support and encouragement

Chapter 1

As usual, it had been a hectic day at the Chapel Street station. The atmosphere had been restrained, but for all the forced jocularity and horseplay, the tension lay like a grey blanket of doom over the entire section. I was directly or indirectly involved in quite a few cases, from auto theft to suicides, domestics, the usual break-and-enters, home invasions and gang-related misdemeanours. And inevitably, the continual drug-related investigations, one of which I was currently involved in. These days, drugs were accepted as being a major factor behind all of the above offences and the driving force behind most of the criminal activity that graced our fair city of Melbourne; a cynical fact of life we accepted as part of what was laughingly referred to as the ongoing and losing battle against crime.

Why the fuck do you care so much? I thought for the thousandth time in my ten-year career as a cop. Because of the fight against injustice, I answered myself, also for the thousandth time. Trying to make even a small dent in the horrors that mankind is capable of is an innate part of your character, dipstick.

I heaved a sigh of relief as I slipped off my skirt, threw it in the corner to join the rest of my uniform, stepped into the tub and sank into the soothing foamy warmth that welcomed and enveloped my stressed and exhausted body. What else would you rather do, join the army? Maybe enrol in Duntroon Military Academy and learn how to impersonally kill and maim total strangers in a far-off foreign land in so-called defence of your country? You're not a killer of strangers, sweetheart, you were born to be a cop, to match your mind against the baddies and bring them to justice and retribution.

The silent inner argument continued until the warm, scented, silky water eventually started to soothe my senses and I willed myself into a peaceful meditative state, my mind escaping into a void of nothingness. That's probably why I didn't hear the sound of my front door being opened or the intruder's footsteps that silently approached with deadly intent towards my closed bathroom door.

It must have been quick because all I can remember is my sudden panic as strong hands grabbed my shoulders and shoved my head under the water and held it there. I must have gasped from the shock, sucking in the soapy water but automatically closing my oesophagus to prevent me from swallowing or breathing in. I struggled desperately, thrashing my legs, my body writhing but unable to escape the force and strength of the unexpected attack.

My attacker's hands slipped on my soapy shoulders and he was forced to change his grip allowing me a brief moment to surface and suck in a mouthful of air, not giving me time to scream but time enough to see his balaclava-covered head and the cold killer eyes through the eye slits before his hands covered my face and he again pushed me under the water and held me there with terrible strength. I tried desperately to grab his fingers and bend them back but they were too slippery. I continued to struggle and even managed to gulp another mouthful of air but that must have really pissed him off because he raised me from the water like a limp rag doll and smashed my head onto the rim of the bath.

Blackness!

Suddenly there was peace. I'd stopped struggling, my mind became filled with an awareness that I had never known before and I felt myself sort of lifting, floating and carefree ... This is

2

amazing, I thought, what's happening here? I was in the bath, someone was drowning me! A dream, I was dreaming! I *am* dreaming! I'd drifted off in the bath with the worries of my job on my mind and had constructed a vivid nightmare. How amazing! Then came the realisation that I was looking down at a woman's body lying in the bath. It felt like I was floating up in the corner of the ceiling, looking down. A man in black jeans and a leather jacket was bending over the woman. He had something on his head, a grey balaclava. As his arms lifted from her body they were covered with soap bubbles. Through the patches of foam I could see his forearms were bare where the sleeves of his jacket had been pushed up, and covered with tattoos: blue and green snakes wrapped around a dagger, Maori symbols, swirls of lines. Very distinctive, quite pretty really, if you liked tattoos.

He rested his hands on the side of the bath, slowly rose to his feet and stood looking down at his handiwork. The woman's face broke the surface of the water. Her eyes were closed and she looked quite peaceful. Her hair wasn't looking too good plastered to her head, with black strands flattened against her cheeks and forehead and blood trickling down the right side of her face from the gash on her head. Her makeup was a bit blurry and streaked but yes, she looked peaceful. I know that face but usually it doesn't look that relaxed. It was always very mobile, laughing a lot, sometimes frowning in deep thought, the brown eyes quick to dart around, taking everything in, and tiny wrinkles at the corners of her eyes. Across the forehead, a little scar on the left cheek where that bastard had hit her when she was a constable on the beat five years ago. The lips were still fairly good though, quite full in repose, as they were now. The lipstick's a bit smudged but a nice shade, Coral Blush.

Mmm, boobs still looking alright. Of course they're looking better because the water is supporting them, I suppose. Skin a bit pale, maybe, but all in all, the body's in pretty good shape. Yes, I can definitely ID this body, there's no doubt about it – it's me!

Detective Sergeant Lucielle Lambert, AKA Lucky Lambert – *never* referred to as Lucielle, which she hates – twenty-nine years of age, currently, or rather recently, stationed at the St Kilda Police Station, 92 Chapel Street, St Kilda Victoria 3182. Ten years in the service, three as a Detective Sergeant, two as Senior Detective Sergeant, ambitious to make it to Superintendent. Fit and healthy, works well with her colleagues but is sometimes thought of as too much of a loner. Clean and respectable record of service with numerous arrests to her credit and copes well with the ribbing from her fellow officers about her ski-slope nose, which they claim is caused by relentlessly keeping it to the grindstone, or sticking it in where it isn't wanted, or by constantly running into too many departmental walls. Has a good sense of humour and can give as good as she gets.

As I pondered, I suddenly had a mental flash of myself as a skinny young girl, riding my pushbike at great speed through the backstreets of Caulfield. I felt again the thrill of the speed and the wind blowing against my face and in my hair; the freedom from constraint. The happiness was intense. I screeched around a corner and into the driveway of our house, braked hard, dismounted, carefully leaned the bike against the wall next to the front door, grabbed my schoolbag, ran up the seven steps, flung open the door and exploded into the living room.

I was met with a sudden, shocked silence and confronted by a startled group of six elegantly dressed women wearing the very latest in smart casual 80s attire. The stench of mixed brands of expensive perfumes and makeup assailed my nostrils mixed with the unmistakeable aroma of imported Italian coffee, hot, freshly baked savoury tarts, and just a hint of fresh strawberry sponge cake and whipped cream; just the ticket for a kid home from a harrowing day at school followed by a couple of strenuous hours of sports.

A sudden gasp of disapproval erupted from my 'dear' mother.

'Lucielle!' she almost screamed in outraged effrontery only controlled by her steely desire to appear socially acceptable in front of her fawning friends. 'You're early, dear,' she said through obviously grated dental implants. 'I thought you were attending your ballet classes this afternoon, darling? Now do go to your room and clean yourself up. I'm sure you have lots of homework to do. You know this is our regular Lauriston Larrikin Old Girls' Wednesday soiree, and children, especially smelly, grubby, unkempt ones,' she added with just the slightest flaring of her nostrils and a rather snide smirk, 'are not invited.'

'Sorry, Mummy, I forgot. And it wasn't ballet, it was rugby practice,' I quipped as I adjusted my panties, which had lodged in a wedgie up my bum. Stealing a savoury tart and half a scone spread with quince jam and an artful dob of whipped cream decorated with chocolate sprinkles, I headed for the safety of my room. I heard the embarrassed, forced titters from the 'clan' as I bolted up the stairs and my mother's voice overriding the laughter.

'Oh, dear, the young girls of today,' she sighed in exasperation. 'They simply have no idea of class or social behaviour. I wouldn't dare enrol her in Lauriston. She wants to become a policewoman, can you believe it? Can you imagine their reaction?'

I slammed the door to my room loudly, cutting off the hateful giggles from the living room.

'What a pack of bitches!'

The flash from my childhood suddenly disappeared and I was aware that my attacker had disappeared. Then I heard a male voice calling from the front door.

'Lucky? You there? It's me and Patricia. We've brought those papers for you to sign. Why did you leave the front door unlocked?'

He then obviously spoke to Patricia, the middle-aged and plump little assistant from his office whom I'd met a few times before at the firm's parties. She'd never impressed me, I must admit: a plain little mouse with terrible, Big W dress sense and the charisma of a slab of lard. I could never understand why he'd hired her; maybe to give an air of respectability to his more conservative clients. All the other female staff he'd hired were long- legged lovelies with pert boobs and bums straight from the pages of *Vogue*. Patricia would have been an excellent advert for *The Biggest Loser*.

'I keep *telling* her not to leave the doors and windows unlocked in this neighbourhood … Lucky?' he again called.

It was Paul, my ex-husband. He'd told me he might be dropping around some papers for me to sign. Timing, Paul, timing.

'I'm in here,' I thought I called, 'stuck up here on the ceiling. Come and get me down.'

But he didn't seem to hear me as I heard him going from room to room calling my name and it was quite a while before Patricia came to the bathroom door and peeped in.

She stopped dead, a look of horror dawning, staring at the body in the bathtub with its arm hanging over the side and the blood from the head gash staining the water. She lifted her hands to her face and let out an ear-shattering scream that didn't wake the dead, unfortunately, and pandemonium broke out.

Paul rushed into the room and stopped suddenly also, staring ashen faced at the body. Patricia kept screaming.

'Oh, God, no. Lucky! Lucky!' he yelled as he rushed to the body. 'What happened, what happened?'

6

Still calling my name, he desperately tried to lift the body from the bath but the slippery weight was too much for him.

'Patricia, give me a hand, she keeps slipping and I can't get a grip!'

But Patricia was obviously paralysed with horror and therefore useless for anything except screaming, the stupid broad.

He felt for a pulse and obviously couldn't find one.

'I'm fine, I'm up here. Something strange has just happened. I'm sort of stuck up here. Get me down.'

But he couldn't seem to hear me. He slapped the dead woman's face a few times, none too gently I might add, and shook her, repeating my name. Patricia, not surprisingly, must have run out of breath because the screams subsided into a series of racking sobs. She covered her face with shaking hands and sank down onto the toilet seat. Paul looked around the tiny bathroom in panic and then stopped and just stared down at the body in the bath for a long while, trying to take it all in.

'Call an ambulance!' he suddenly yelled at Patricia but she was frozen to the toilet seat, so overcome with shock, she couldn't move.

Realising she wasn't going to be of much help, he turned and rushed out into the living room.

It was hard to tell but there seemed to be a long pause while Patricia continued to whimper uncontrollably. Time seemed to have stopped or at least, slowed down, and then I heard his voice shouting into the telephone.

'Hello? Ambulance! … This is Paul Lambert. I need an ambulance. My wife, my ex-wife, seems to have drowned in the bath tub. She must have slipped and hit her head. There's a lot of blood. She's not breathing. I can't feel a pulse. Please send someone immediately!'

7

He stumbled over the address, mistakenly giving the address of his own apartment and then, suddenly correcting himself, gave them mine. There was a pause and I thought he'd hung up but then he said in a slightly more restrained manner, 'Look, I'd better tell you, she's a Senior Detective Sergeant at the St Kilda Police Station, Lucielle Lambert. They'll have to be notified … Thank you … Right … Right, yes, I understand … No, I can't do that. I can't seem to get her out of the bath … Okay, I'll try again, but please hurry!'

He hung up and there was silence apart from Patricia's pathetic sniffling. He didn't return to the bathroom.

Well, this is nice, I thought, I'm obviously dead and stuck up here on the bloody ceiling with a useless husband doing God knows what in the living room, probably hitting my Scotch, and a bloody useless, sobbing woman propped up on my loo. You'd think Paul would ve checked more thoroughly; tried a bit of CPR; something. He could've thrown a towel over me to help him get a grip and pull me out. No, he panicked. He just checked my pulse, couldn't find one, slapped me around a bit and that was it. He's such a hopeless wimp; pretty, but a wimp. No wonder I ditched him. Bloody lawyers. Never think of the obvious in an emergency.

Now, having time to get things into perspective, I checked myself over. I was feeling fine, perfectly calm; in fact the best I'd ever felt. I tried to look down at my body, well, the one I was sure I was wearing now, and it was just a sort of glowing, translucent copy of the body I was used to, the one lying dead in the bathtub. It didn't seem important. It was sort of what I expected, in a way.

So this is death. So the believers in an afterlife were right, after all. And I'd rubbished the idea. Just goes to show you. Won't the world be surprised? But then I thought, wait a minute,

I can't tell them. No one seems to be able to see or hear me. A ghost? I'm a bloody ghost! A spook! Well, bugger me! Cool!

So where's this 'white light' I'm supposed to see? Where's the bloody tunnel? Everything looks like it did before only the colours and shapes are a bit brighter, clearer somehow.

I heard the ambulance arrive and saw the medics rushing around attending to the body, trying to revive it, gently leading Patricia out.

'Looks like she's gone,' one of them said.

'No I haven't,' I yelled. 'I'm up here!' But of course they couldn't hear me.

Peter, one of the young constables I recognised from the station, had been standing in the doorway; he stepped forward and looked at the body.

'Accident?' he asked the attendant.

'No, it wasn't a bloody accident,' I yelled. 'I was murdered! Big bloke, in a balaclava – Tattoos! Get Homicide over here, you young idiot.'

The attendant nodded. 'Looks like it. Must've slipped getting in or out of the bath.' He pointed to the gash on the body's head. 'Nasty gash.'

'What do you expect? He whacked my head on the bloody bath!'

'Was the front door open when the husband arrived?'

' No, he said it was closed but not locked,' came the reply.

'I'll ring it in,' the young cop muttered as he turned back to the living room. 'See what they want to do.'

Without thinking, I decided to follow him and get his attention somehow, and the strangest thing happened. I could follow him! I floated through the wall and into the living room! This is really cool. God, it was a bit of a mess for entertaining. How embarrassing. Bits of clothing and underwear, magazines, dirty coffee cups, the dried-out remain of yesterday's pizza.

Paul was sitting in my leather wing-back chair with his head in his hands. He was looking his usual sartorial self and definitely out of place in a messy flat in Elsternwick. He was wearing a dark grey Peter Morrissey suit, mauve shirt and matching silk tie. He would've looked more at home in a court room where he could charm the women jurors. He certainly knew how to dress and he was certainly gorgeous, with his dark brown hair, brown eyes and slim, languid, muscled body. But, as it turned out, he was compelled to share himself around. Why should he deprive other women of his beauty and sex appeal when it was so under-used by a wife who was addicted to her job and worked all sorts of strange shift hours? I suppose he had a point. Patricia, on the other hand, had been deposited on the cream sofa where she lay with a black cushion under her head looking like a small, beached humpback.

Paul looked up as the constable entered.

'Well?' he asked tentatively.

The young constable shook his head sadly. 'Sorry,' he said. 'They'll get her to the hospital but …'

Paul sighed and dropped his head again.

'I'll have to phone it in,' the cop said as he took out his mobile phone.

'Tell 'em to send the Homicide boys,' I said, but of course he couldn't hear me. Frustrated, I slammed my fist onto the coffee table but my hand seemed to go straight through!

He got on to Brian, one of my colleagues, made the usual accidental-death report and described the situation as he wandered back into the bathroom.

Well, at least Paul seemed very upset and agitated as he stood up and wandered around the room. He picked up a framed photo of us both from happier times and stared at it. Damn, I'd meant to throw that bloody photo out. It was a shot of us taken in a restaurant just after we were married. God, how young and happy we both looked. I thought we were. Until I found out he was carrying on a bit of ex-marital skinny dipping with that Olympic swimming candidate and possibly other extra connubial distractions.

'Why couldn't you just let it go, Lucky?' he mumbled as he looked at the photo and shook his head sadly.

Let go? Let go? I fumed. She was supposed to be the breaststroker, not you! And it turned out you were the breaststroker and she was a cockstroker! Get over it, Paul, I don't do double acts with freestylers, either. I'm strictly a one-on-one kind of event. No, you did one deep dive too many, sonny.

The attendants carried the body out to the ambulance on a gurney. I watched dispassionately, feeling no real connection anymore. A group of ghoulish neighbours stood around watching and chatting like they were discussing an episode of *Neighbours*. Paul and Patricia, who had been manhandled to her feet by the ambulance attendants and the constable, followed out the front door and I was suddenly alone, haunting my own apartment. I floated from room to room wondering what I could do to get people to believe that I'd been murdered. The killer had left no clues, no footprints, nothing to suggest he had even been there.

The door. The front door. They said it had been left unlocked! I never left it unlocked. Paul knew that. I automatically locked it whenever I went out or came back in. It was a habit I had. How had he got in? I flew to the door to examine it. There were no signs of forced entry. Had he picked the lock? No, it was a deadlock; you had to have a key. Where did he get a key to my apartment?

I drifted down onto the couch to think. Not that it made any difference; I couldn't feel the couch so I could've just floated

11

around. But it gave me a sense of familiarity, I suppose, and in my present state I needed all the familiarity I could get.

Who actually had a key to my apartment? I suppose the estate agent I rented it through, and there was a copy back at the station in case of emergency. Who else? Paul? Did I give him a copy? I doubted it but I did lend it to him a few weeks back when I had the flu and he'd insisted on coming around to look after me. I'd resisted, of course, but it was during one of his contrite, forgive-me-please, take-me-back, it's-really-you-I-love periods and I was just too sick to argue. But he had given it back as soon as I was on deck again. Actually he'd nursed me very well, feeding and bathing me, running errands, chatting about my work. Anyway, I was sure it wasn't Paul who drowned me. First of all, he wasn't dressed for it and secondly, he wouldn't have the guts and he was much slimmer and weaker than the guy who attacked me. On top of that he didn't have a motive. What the hell *was* the motive? And what can I do about it now? I really need some help, here, I'm desperate.

I suddenly heard a voice in my mind. 'Then ask,' it said.

'Ask who?' I replied to myself. 'God?'

'It's worth a shot,' came the voice again.

Now, it wasn't as if I was an atheist. I mean, I certainly wasn't a church goer or a believer in any sort of religion. Being a cop and seeing all the violence and injustice and unanswered prayers put a stop to that but I suppose there was a biological need to believe in something. Maybe that was why I meditated. I'd always believed I had a higher self, or an over-self, or was it an inner self? A part of me that was connected to some sort of Universal Consciousness that my physical body just couldn't reach without meditating; clearing my mind of the prattle of insignificant, daily thoughts and just letting go. I must subconsciously believe there is something out there that can help. Meditating certainly relaxed me and I remember many times when I was facing some sort of crisis, I had unintentionally called out for help, like soldiers do on the battlefield. After all, there are no atheists on the battlefield.

Like the time I almost drowned in the local pool when I was learning to swim and Joey Thornton appeared out of nowhere and had jumped in and saved me. Mind you, I originally thought it was just an excuse to get his hands on my boobs, such as they were at eight years old. Many times when I had some problem on my mind I had meditated on some sort of answer or direction and strangely the answer had come. I had initially put it down to my subconscious working it out for me, but sometimes that didn't explain it; like people I 'accidentally' ran into who set me off in another direction, or something I read in a book I just happened to pick up that helped me make a decision. I'd witnessed some strange, inexplicable phenomena in my time on the force but the concept of a personal God who cared or even gave a stuff about people or the world didn't rattle my chains. I suppose I was an agnostic if I had to put a name to it. I believed there was something out there but I had no idea what.

So if I'm an agnostic, maybe I should find out if there is a meaning to all this. I mean, I've certainly proved there's life at the end of the tunnel, so to speak, so maybe, just maybe …

'Ask,' the voice urged again.

I tried to clear my mind of any distractions like I did when I meditated and I guess it was the same as praying when I focused and summoned up all my strength and willpower and said, 'Hey, I need some help here!'

Chapter 2

Everything seemed to go hazy. My surroundings started to fade and I was aware of complete darkness to my left side but a growing brightness to my right. The darkness on the left was complete, almost solid, and I sensed revulsion emanating from it. It reminded me of being alone at night in the corridors of a prison when the inmates had gone to sleep, only much worse, much more evil. That was the only word for it: evil. I sensed beings or monsters in the darkness and there was no way I was going anywhere near that, thank you.

The light on my right grew in intensity and slowly formed into a sort of swirling, cloudy, golden luminescence that transposed itself into a sort of tunnel. And far down the tunnel was the brightest white light I had ever seen.

The tunnel! The white light! There it is! It's the tunnel. It's true! Well, I'll be buggered.

I suddenly felt as if I was being sucked into this vortex of light. I seemed to be travelling at great speed but there was no sense of wind or propulsion. I wasn't alone. There seemed to be other beings or a presence around me emitting the most wonderful sense of safety and unconditional love but I couldn't see them. It was the most amazing experience I had ever had. It was like flying down a never-ending path of love that was leading me home.

A group of figures appeared at the end of the tunnel, walking towards me. I couldn't discern any features except I could pick the outlines of men and women. As they drew near I was struck by an even greater force of love and acceptance and I could now start detecting hazy sort-of features. A tall man stepped out of the rank and came closer. The first thing that struck me was his eyes. They were a startlingly clear, deep blue that seemed to look into me with the gentlest smile I have ever seen; like an old friend meeting with me after a long absence. My mind added more detail and I now saw that he had short, black, curly hair that framed a strong, chiselled face and the muscled physique of a Greek god. And then I noticed to my surprise, he was indeed wearing a short, white, draped sort of sleeveless tunic with a cowl neck, reminiscent of the sculptures of Greek gods or warriors I'd seen in the Athens museum. A tan, embossed leather belt circled his waist drawing attention to his lean, muscled chest and he wore a heavy gold chain bracelet around his wrist. Wow, what a hottie!

He smiled even more broadly and if I had a heart it would have skipped.

'Hello, Lucielle,' I heard him say, although I'm sure his sensuous mouth never moved. 'Welcome home.'

'Thank you, but who are you?' I asked, but my mouth didn't seem to move either. It was as if we were exchanging thoughts.

'Who would you like me to be?' he asked with a mischievous grin.

A sudden shock ran through me.

'You're not … I mean, you wouldn't be … you aren't … *God*, are you? I mean you look so young and,' I just stopped myself from thinking, gorgeous. 'And you can't be … Jesus … are you?'

God, I hope he's not. A stream of pictures of things I'd rather forget stampeded through my mind. 'I mean, you don't look like any of his pictures … And,' I blundered on unable to control the torrent of guilty thoughts racing through my mind, 'you're certainly dressed differently … I mean, he always has a long robe and a beard and he looks sort of Jewish … with a beard,' I added lamely.

This time he actually laughed. He then turned and called, 'Judith?'

One of the female characters detached herself from the group and in a second she was standing by our side. She appeared to be a rather lovely, blonde in her early twenties.

'Judith, tell Lucielle what you think I look like.'

'Why, you're a little, grey-haired, elderly man with a bald head and big ears, just like my father was in my last incarnation. You have a little pot tummy, too, which makes you look very jolly. And I love you so much.'

'Thank you, Judith, and I love you too as I always will.'

'Judith' disappeared in a flash back into the group and I was standing there like a confused, chastised young kid. He smiled again and I was aware of his stunning white teeth.

'You see, Lucielle, I appear to you just as you would like me to appear.'

'But what's your name? I mean, what do I call you?'

'Wasn't it your Shakespeare who said, "what's in a name?" What would you like to call me?'

This is rather fun, I thought. I have no idea what's going on here but everything feels so … right. If this is a dream I don't think I want to wake up just yet.

'It's not a dream, Lucielle, this is reality,' he said with a sudden, serious, meaningful look.

Joseph, I suddenly thought, I'd like to think of you as Joseph.

'Then, Joseph I will be to you,' he smiled.

Not the one from the Bible, I quickly thought.

He laughed uproariously. 'Walk with me,' he said, as he gestured further up the path.

The rest of the group seemed to have disappeared and we began to walk. Now there's a strange thing, I thought, I can't see our feet. It hadn't occurred to me before and it was a bit of a shock. Our legs seemed to disappear from the calf down. They seemed to disappear in a sort of haze. But, another strange thing: I was now dressed in my police uniform. Well, at least I didn't arrive naked as I was the last time I saw my body. That could have been a bit embarrassing.

'I can't see our feet,' I said. 'Don't tell me we're actually walking on clouds.'

He roared with laughter again.

'No, we don't really need to see our feet because we're not actually walking as you did before. It's just nice for you to relate to the sense of walking; it helps you to relax while you become adjusted.'

Uh huh, I thought, well, you can certainly say that again.

'Your favourite flowers are waterlilies and irises, right?'

'Well, you have done your homework, haven't you,' I replied.

'Look around you,' he said.

I lifted my head and did as he suggested. As I took in our surroundings, I was astounded to see the pathway now wound around a beautiful pond filled with the most glorious waterlilies and on the edges were clumps of beautiful irises. Lush green hills appeared in the distance. The sky was so blue and clear. The colours were intense and alive, glowing from what appeared to be an inner life or energy. I stopped and stared in amazement.

A thought suddenly occurred to me.

'Are you what some people refer to as my "spiritual guide"? Is that why you met me?'

He nodded. 'Yes. I've guided you for most of your life in the other realm.'

'Well, weren't you supposed to protect me? I mean, how come you didn't protect me from being murdered? Where were you when I needed you? Was it your day off? Or were you attending an angel convention or something?'

He smiled that smile again.

'Lucielle, there's only so much we can do. Don't forget free will. The person who took the life from you also had free will. It was his decision.'

'But if we all have a guide, why didn't his guide stop him?'

'His guide would've tried to warn him but like the majority of human beings your killer wasn't listening. He was closed off from his guide or his higher self. He chose to make a decision based on his lower mental intelligence, his immediate needs or desires. He wasn't capable of seeing the consequences either to you or to himself. Unfortunately, that happens in the vast majority of cases in mankind. They choose to ignore the moral spiritual advice that is always there to help them. We can't get through to them if they don't choose to listen.'

'But what about "a time to live and a time to die"? Are you saying it was my time? It was my fate to be bashed and drowned? I was young and healthy. I should've had years more to live. There was so much more for me to do, to achieve.'

There was a long pause, as if he was trying to think of how he could explain in a way that I could understand.

'And you will, if you choose to. Just because you leave your earthly body doesn't mean that that's the end of everything. It's actually a beginning. You must realise that, now you're here. Your soul doesn't just stop and float around in eternity, sitting on a cloud, dressed in a flowing gown with a pair of beautiful feathered wings and strumming a harp,' he said. 'Well, you could of course, I suppose, if that is what you really want, but you'll see there are many opportunities and choices still to make. Time, as you were used to it, doesn't really exist in reality. In your Earth-conditioned way of thinking, time is lateral, judged by creation and gradual decay and eventually death, but that is not so in reality. You have the chance to continue along many pathways that have innumerable opportunities to develop, to learn, to experience. To answer your question, immediately your body was killed, it was your time to die, but it was also your time to continue.'

Hmm. Now that was something for me to think about.

'So, what would you like to achieve?' he asked.

'I want to know who killed me and why.'

He nodded as if that was what he expected me to say.

'Then so you shall. Let's go.'

'Go where?'

'We have a department here called the CIA.'

'The CIA?' I said in astonishment, 'You're joking.'

He laughed.

'No, not that one – that one certainly wasn't made in Heaven. No, you're going to the Celestial Investigation Agency.'

Now it was my turn to laugh.

'You are joking!'

'No, we have a department that helps with investigations into crimes of all sorts here. We try to lead the authorities to solve crimes. But again, they have to be open to our suggestions.'

'So you mean you actually know who it was who murdered me?'

'Yes, of course.'

'Well, tell me!'

He shook his head. 'That's not how it works here. It's up to you to find the answer. It's part of your training, your development.'

Oh, shit, I thought. No rest for the wicked.

'You weren't all that wicked,' he laughed.

'Oops, sorry about that,' I said.

I really have to put a brake on my language or thoughts up here, I thought.

'So I don't get any Heavenly help or advice?'

He shrugged. 'Only if you really deserve it. You were a very talented detective. Use your talents just as you would in the other dimension. But you do have a more advanced data base here.'

'How do you mean?'

Suddenly we were in a sort of office. It reminded me of many other police station offices I'd been in, only much bigger. Other officers and uniformed personnel worked at desks and floated around with files in their hands, looking busy. They nodded in a friendly sort of way as I entered and one young constable pointed me towards a desk that had the usual paraphernalia on it including what looked like a computer monitor.

'Hi,' said an older plain-clothes cop at the next desk. 'I'm Terry, welcome to the madhouse.'

'Hi, I'm Senior Detective Sergeant Lucky Lambert. Is that where I am, in a madhouse?' It wouldn't have surprised me.

He laughed.

'Well, not exactly. It just seems that way sometimes. Just arrive?' he asked.

'Yes,' I replied, 'and I'm not sure about what to do next.'

'Got a particular case in mind?' he asked.

'Yes, my murder,' I replied.

'Ah, tricky one. Any suspects?'

'No, not a clue. Some perp broke into my flat, bashed and drowned me. I couldn't recognise him because he was wearing a balaclava over his head.'

'Any clues left?'

I shook my head.

'Motives?'

'None that I can think of yet.'

'Hmm. Well, obviously someone had it in for you. I'd check through some of your old cases, see if that comes up with anything.'

'Good idea.' I was suddenly at a loss as to just how to accomplish that.

'Just how do I go about that?' I asked.

'The Akashic Web,' Terry replied, gesturing to the monitor on my desk.

'Akashic Web? What the hell is the Akashic Web?'

'It's sort of like the Internet only on a broader scale; sort of based on the Web of Life. Very helpful. Just go on line like you would usually do.'

Amazed, I studied the monitor in front of me and noticed a logo marked A.W.

I clicked on it and sure enough, up came the website! I typed in, Lucielle (Lucky) Lambert, and hit the search button. Instantly, there it was! My own website! Wow! This was the fastest broadband speed I've ever come across.

The page had a lovely blue background with white and gold writing and very artistic graphics of clouds. At the top of the page was a photograph of me in my uniform; one of my better photos, I thought. Thank God it wasn't the one the forensic guys took of my body in the bath. One of the links said 'Biography', and I just couldn't resist. I clicked on it and up came a video of my entire life.

My God, it was in 3D.

Chapter 3

There I was as a baby, just being born. My mother was screaming, of course. My beautiful father was standing by with the most wonderfully proud grin on his face, happy tears streaming down his face.

'Arthur,' Mum screamed, 'I am NEVER going through this again! Do you understand? Never! From now on you're moving into the guest room.'

'Oh, Helen, all new mothers say that. You'll forget all about it in a little while. Just look at her, she gorgeous! I'm so proud of you.'

I remember how bright it was and actually experienced the wonderful feeling of that first breath.

After that, the video seemed to speed up and took me through my whole life from childhood until that last moment when that terrible man held me under the water. I saw the friends I'd made and the wonderful times we'd shared and the love I felt for them and them for me. I saw every decision I'd made and the results, some good, some not so good; the anger I'd felt, the unintentional suffering I'd inflicted. I saw and felt the positive and negative reactions my actions had on other people; the hurt I'd caused, sometimes without realising it; the unconditional love I'd been given; the tears I'd shed; the laughter and happiness; the silly feuds and arguments that didn't seem to matter now when I saw them in context.

I saw episodes with my mother, with whom I'd never got on and considered very shallow and inconsequential. But I suddenly understood why she chose to act that way. I sensed that she did love me but was afraid to show it. She'd lost her parents when she was only very young and feared losing anything she loved so she adopted a brittle persona of self-protection. I felt so warmly my father's love and saw in him my personal spiritual retreat.

It was an amazing experience, sometimes deeply harrowing, sometimes joyous. But the distressing times didn't last for long because I felt an understanding that this was a negative emotion quickly replaced by a feeling of great Love. Occasionally, the camera seemed to zoom in on a particular event, sometimes a seemingly unimportant event, like seeing myself as a child and lost in the study and wonder of a butterfly; the way it sat on a leaf, completely indifferent to me and my presence; the love I'd felt for this beautiful creature with its fragile blue and yellow translucent wings. The seemingly insignificant became significant.

At the end of my life review, a line of dialogue appeared on the screen:

Any Questions ?

Well, there were certainly many but I thought I needed the time to really absorb the experience so I typed, 'I'll get back to you on that.'

I hit the Backspace button and returned to the main page.

I then clicked on my case files logo and started to review the cases I'd been involved in, searching for a clue as to why I'd been murdered. I was staggered at just how many there were. I read the most recent ones and discarded them because none of them seemed to present a strong motive for my death.

Suddenly I was aware of a presence standing behind me, looking over my shoulder. I heard a man's voice say, 'Senior Detective Sergeant Lambert?'

I turned and was amazed to see a young, good-looking constable standing there, smiling. He was tall, with fair curly hair and an angelic face. Well, he would have, wouldn't he? But then I recognised him.

'Tony? Tony Buchanan? Is that really you?'

'It sure is, ma'am,' he replied with that cheeky grin he always seemed to have plastered on his handsome face.

'What the hell are you doing here, constable?'

'I seem to be a permanent resident, ma'am, a sort of eternal posting.'

'What happened?'

'Well, I was trout fishing on my day off and I must've slipped and hit my head on a rock and drowned. The next thing I knew, here I am.'

'Oh, I'm sorry, Tony, you were such a sweetie and so good at your job. We did a few cases when we were on the beat together, didn't we?'

'We sure did, ma'am. We were great partners.'

'We certainly were.'

'You working on another case now?'

'As a matter of fact, yes. You see, I was murdered and I haven't got a clue who did it or the motive. I've just been checking on a few case histories to see if I can come up with something.'

I explained all that had happened to get me here while he listened patiently, nodding his head.

'And you're not getting any help from your guide?'

I suddenly remembered Joseph and realised he seemed to have disappeared when I arrived at the station.

'Apparently not,' I said. 'It seems I'm supposed to work it out for myself – part of the training, I assume.'

'Yeah, that seems to happen a lot,' he agreed. 'Are you out for revenge?'

Well, that sort of staggered me.

'I don't think so,' I replied, uncertainly. 'I like to think of it as justice.'

He suddenly became very serious. 'Your justice or a higher power justice; one of the top echelons up here? Like a Heavenly Commissioner?'

I couldn't answer that one.

'Maybe it's just that I hate a messy case. I like to get the answers. I'm not the judge. I don't dish out the punishment.'

'Hmm,' he said. 'You like some help?'

'That'd be great,' I said. 'If you haven't got anything else on.'

'No, I'm just hanging around, so to speak, or rather, floating. So let's see what we've got to work on.'

He seemed to pull up a spare seat and sat next to me, peering at the monitor.

'Well, you've been working on this drug supply case, how far have you got with that?'

'Not far, I'm afraid. I did think I had a lead when one of my informers rang me to arrange a meeting. But when I got to the location I found him stoned out of his brain and breathing his last. He'd been knocked down by a hit and run. All he managed to say at the end was something about it being closer than I thought and to watch my ... and that was all. I guess the gang found out he was informing and shut him down.'

'Watch your back, maybe?' Tony mused. 'Closer than you think? You don't think he was talking about a crooked cop?'

I shrugged. I was always watching my back in my trade. Well, almost always, I thought, remembering how I'd been killed.

'Hey, remember this one?' Tony pointed to an old case that had happened years ago. 'We worked on this one together.'

'That was way back when I was only a constable,' I said. 'Oops, no offence, Constable.'

He smiled. 'None taken, Detective Sergeant,' deliberately omitting the 'Senior' as I had done with him. He continued staring at the screen. 'It was a domestic. Some bloke had blown

25

his stack and beaten up his wife, almost killed her. I remember as soon as we rang the bell, she flung open the door and ran out screaming, straight into my arms. She was a very beautiful girl, too. Well, she was before her husband got to work on her.'

'Yes, I do remember that. He went berserk. He kept yelling "this is a private argument between husband and wife. Get the fuck out of our lives. Mind your own fucking business. You bastards are always sticking your noses in to innocent peoples' lives. I'll get you mongrels one day, etc etc." He obviously had previous and he thought it was his right to treat his wife any way he wanted; usual scenario. The bastard went for me and I had a hell of a job controlling him. In fact, I think he was responsible for the scar on my cheek.'

'What scar?' Tony looked at my face. 'There's no scar there now. Your face is perfect.'

Can a young angelic constable blush? It certainly looked like it or was that my ego shining through?

'What happened to the husband?' I asked, trying to diffuse an awkward moment.

'We arrested him and he was tried for aggravated assault and drug dealing. We testified, remember? They uncovered a quantity of cocaine, angel dust and a cocktail of other stuff from a tip off. The stuff was hidden in a hole under the fireplace. Scott was his name, Scott Warner; he was tied in with some bikie gang.' He checked the screen again. 'The Rusty Pistons.'

'The Rusty Piss Tins?'

Tony laughed.

'No, Pistons, like in an engine. Of course we knew he was also involved in drug distribution somehow but we could never get onto his supplier,' he continued. 'How deep he was in we couldn't establish. There was the usual code of silence. Apparently, he reckoned his wife had been sampling the merchandise too much and he wasn't happy about it. He claimed he warned her to lay off but she ignored him so he started bashing her up. She must've been snorting most of the profits. He claimed he wasn't a user, just a supplier, reckoned the stuff would kill you.'

'Ha, so he bashed her up because he didn't approve of her using drugs? Supplying was alright but not using? Now is that weird thinking or am I being cynical?'

Tony laughed.

'It takes all sorts, Detective Sergeant. Anyway, she'd had enough and got herself a lawyer and charged him with assault. He was sent down for five years. She hit the witness stand and opened up about his drug dealing and how he continually bashed her up and then screamed bloody murder because he only got five years. She claimed he'd got her hooked on the stuff. It was all his fault.'

'Lucielle?' I heard the voice and recognised it immediately. Tony seemed to immediately disappear and in his place, standing behind his chair, was my mother!

'Mum?' I turned to her, startled. 'What the hell are you doing here?'

'Hello, dear, sorry to disturb you. I know you hate me bothering you at the office but I'd thought I'd look in on you, see how you're doing.'

'Mum, you shouldn't be here,' I said, looking around at the other officers who seemed to be ignoring us. Then it suddenly occurred to me. 'Mum, you aren't, you know, you haven't died, have you?'

She laughed but it was not her usual patronising laugh, it actually seemed to amuse her.

'I mean,' I stumbled on, 'you didn't die of shock when you heard about me being attacked?'

Fat chance of that I thought.

27

'No, of course not, dear. I knew you'd look after yourself. You always have without any interference from me. No, I'm astral-travelling. I mean, I could be just dreaming but apparently I often astral-travel in my dreams so don't be upset.'

Upset? I was absolutely staggered. The only astral travelling I ever thought she did was in the Astral Taxi Company to the beauty parlour for a quick dye job, facial, manicure and the odd nip and tuck.

'I'm not upset, just a trifle surprised.'

She laughed again in delight.

'Oh, that's nice, dear, I didn't think I could ever surprise you again. Well, how are you? Settling in well? You seem to be. I mean, back at your desk, fiddling around with your blessed files. I wouldn't have imagined there'd be much crime to clear up here.'

'You'd be surprised,' I said trying to get my head around this new development. 'Crime knows no boundaries it seems; murder, robberies, extortion, gang warfare, terrorism …'

'Yes, but terrorism is more of a religious crime, isn't it? I thought Jesus would look after that end of it. Oh yes, I see your point. You investigate the Muslim suicide-bombers? Well, I must say, that's very worthwhile. Send them off to their waiting twenty-four virgins, dear. But make sure they're fat and ugly and toothless. No, not toothless,' she added as an afterthought, 'that might appeal to them.'

I had never heard my mother crack an even slightly off-colour joke before. Maybe that's what happens up here; you lose any false inhibitions.

'Mum, I haven't quite worked out the procedures yet but in the meantime I'm learning what's expected of me and how to go about it. There are different rules that apply here, different laws.'

'Yes, well, there would be, wouldn't there? I mean, what is it people say, "Heaven knows"? Well, sometimes it might know but it's not saying anything until the perpetrators arrive up here. Anyway, don't fret yourself, dear. I know you'll overcome all of your problems; you always do. You always know what's best for people, don't you? Not always best for their emotional problems, of course; everything's always cut and dried with you, black and white. Do the crime, do the time, isn't that what you always say?'

Here we go again.

'What do you mean, "cut and dried, black and white"? I always try to see the other person's point of view. I always try to put myself in their position.'

'Before you make up your mind what's best for them, you mean.'

'No, that's not true! I weigh up the evidence and then I act on it.'

'Regardless of what they feel about it, you mean.'

'Stop trying to tell me what I mean!'

'Sorry, dear.' She seemed to be patting me on the shoulder. 'Things haven't changed, have they?' She seemed a little disappointed. 'I thought when you died, everybody became more – you know, holy and understanding, more spiritual. You know, like angels are supposed to be. But then again, maybe you aren't an angel.' A solution suddenly came to her addled brain. 'Maybe you're in Purgatory. Yes, that must be it; it seems a bit nicer than I imagined Hell to be. Décor's more – tasteful, no fire and brimstone.'

'Mum, just because you die, it doesn't necessarily mean your personality changes and you become all sweetness and light. Why should it? It's just a continuation in a different dimension. I'll admit there's more awareness, but what you do with it is up to yourself. But you do suddenly know what's good for you and what's not.'

And I suddenly felt that what was happening between us wasn't good for either of us.

'Oh? What a pity. We've always had trouble understanding each other, haven't we? I mean, like when you decided to be a policewoman instead of having a respectable career in music or art.'

'Mum, having a respectable career in music or art doesn't pay enough to be independent and have food on the table, let alone wine. And understanding each other has to work on both sides.'

I suddenly remembered my life review and what had shaped her life and felt guilty for upsetting her instead of trying to love her and understand the hard times she'd been through; a lot of it because of me, I was sure.

'Let's forget all about that,' I said trying to change the subject. 'How have you been keeping?'

Now that was a mistake, because she was going to tell me.

'Well, I still miss Arthur, of course. But my friends have been marvellous. They keep me grounded.'

Grounded? In self-pity and self-interest? I wanted to say, but I held my tongue, or rather, kept my thoughts to myself. Missing her husband, my father? I think she was relieved when he died and left her so comfortably off. She was never a companion to him from what I remembered. She was never going to change, she was comfortable in her self-deception and unless Jesus himself appeared to her while she was astral-travelling and gave her a good talking to, she wasn't going to change. Even then she'd probably argue with him and tell him Christianity had gone to the dogs since he left and ask why he hadn't done something about it.

Speaking of my father, I suddenly noticed he was standing in the back of the room watching and listening! I was so thrilled to see him I wanted to call out to him, rush over and hug him, but he smiled and shook his head, placing his finger up to his mouth indicating not to say anything. In my mind I heard him say, 'You and me, later.' I looked at Mum to see if she'd heard but there was no indication she had. Not surprising really; Mum only heard what was in her own mind.

'And what are you working on at the moment, dear,' she asked.

'A murder, actually,' I replied, 'mine.'

'Oh dear yes, that was a terrible shock,' she responded, rather disinterestedly I imagined, then the word 'murder' seemed to sink in and she was shocked, 'Murder? But I thought it was an accident. I thought you hit your head on the bath and drowned. I must admit I thought you must have had one glass of wine too many; well, you did like the odd tipple, didn't you?' She obviously couldn't take in the enormity of the fact. 'But murder – are you sure?

'Yes, Mum, I'm sure, I was there. A big bloke I'd never seen before, wearing a balaclava, broke in, bashed my head on the side of the bath and then drowned me.'

'But that's terrible,' she said, now obviously distressed. 'But why do *you* have to solve it? Are you trying to tell me they don't already know up here who did it?'

'Well, if they do they sure aren't telling me,' I ahrugged.

'But that's ridiculous. I mean, you have a right to know.'

'Maybe so, but it appears that's the way it's got to be.'

'But aren't you getting any help?'

'Well, I've just been talking to a young colleague of mine from the old days and he's offered to help.'

'You don't need another policeman,' she scoffed, and then a brilliant idea occurred to her. 'What you need is a good psychic, a clairvoyant. Now I may be able to help you there: Magda Vollansky. I've had a lot of success with her. She predicted your father's death – well, not in so many words. She said I should get used to living on my own. And Miriam's back problems,' she continued without taking breath, 'she predicted those and she warned Patsy about getting a chest infection, which she did, the very next winter. The girls think she's marvellous. Of course, she was wrong about Claudine getting pregnant. Well, Claudine is getting on but she did start developing tummy aches but they turned out to be flatulence. Magda claims to have an eighty percent success rate.'

If I could have sighed, I would have but it certainly felt like a sigh as I said, 'Mum, you know what I think about that malarkey, they're a con. They take advantage of people's mental state and ask clever questions and give answers that are vague and easily interpretive. I think I'll stick to the acceptable lines of investigation'.

'Suit yourself, dear,' she said, looking a little hurt. 'I was only trying to help.'

Her expression suddenly changed as if she'd suddenly remembered something. 'Oh, I must be off, I have to get back into my body before I wake up. The jolt of re-entry sometimes brings on one of my headaches. Toodle-oo, dear, stay in touch. I do miss your occasional phone calls. And do think about Magda – remember there's more than one way to skin a dingo.'

And with that she was gone.

Chapter 4

Tony suddenly reappeared.

'Hey, I just found out the pathology results from your autopsy have just come in. They discovered welts around your neck and shoulders and there's a suspicion it could be murder. Isn't that great?'

'Well, thank God for that. Now we may get a bit of action. Who's in charge of the case, do you know?'

'Superintendent Blake, Homicide.'

'Well, Blake's not the greatest officer. We can only hope he gets a good result. Is there any way we can keep an eye on him, see how he's progressing?'

'Sure. I've been told we just will ourselves down there and hang out.'

'You mean, haunt the place?'

'Well, sort of. They won't be able to see or hear us, of course, but we may be able to influence them in some way or at least find out what they're doing. I'm not experienced in it, I haven't actually done it myself, but it's worth a try, don't you think?'

'It sure is, Constable. How do we go about it?'

He looked unsure of himself and then Terry appeared and butted in.

'You have to focus on the location and the person you want to see and will yourself there. But you have to get permission from his guide to enter his space. The guides are very protective so you'll have to make a good case. If you get in it's very difficult to interfere. You may not be able to achieve much. You may only be able to see and hear what's going on and that's about all.

And you'll be able to hear conversations and that's always a help.'

A thought suddenly occurred to me.

'Can we will ourselves to the killer's location?'

'You'll have to identify him first and then you might be lucky. Again it depends on his guide. It might have future implications. Access might be denied.'

'Like how?'

'Well, the murderer, through his own free will, may have set himself on a certain path which might not be changeable because it will affect interconnecting paths of other people.'

'Right,' I said, not having a clue what he was talking about.

'Well, Tony,' I said, turning to him, 'you willing to take a shot at it? Ready for an adventure?'

He looked a trifle dubious and not all that confident but he nodded.

'Ready when you are, Detective Sergeant.'

'Okay, let's focus on where we're going and summon up all the willpower we can.'

Suddenly we were flying at great speed, it seemed, through glorious colours of brilliant lights and sounds and within seconds we were hovering over the familiar sight of the St Kilda Police Station.

'Wow!' Tony exclaimed happily. 'What a ride! That was better than the roller coaster at Luna Park!'

'Now, how do we actually get in,' I wondered.

Suddenly a presence appeared beside us. He was also dressed in a police uniform; that of an older Senior Detective Sergeant, but obviously of a higher rank than either of us. So this must be one of the guides.

'And what can I do for you young people?'

'We want to sit in on an investigation being headed by Superintendent Blake,' I replied.

'And why would you be wanting to do that, young lady?'

'Well, he's investigating my murder and I'd like to see how he's getting on.'

'Your murder? A cop killer on the loose? Hmm, don't like that. Can you identify this killer?'

'Well, no, actually. He crept up behind me and drowned me in my bath. I didn't get to see his face. He was wearing a balaclava.'

'Well, I'll tell you what, I'll let you sit in, or rather float in and have a look at what's going on, but a warning, young lady, you are not to interfere in any way. You won't be able to touch anything, of course. They won't be able to hear or see you and as none of them seem to be psychically tuned in, you won't even be able to ask questions. Is that clear?'

I nodded gratefully and flashed him my most winsome smile, which was probably a waste of time anyway.

The next second we were hovering over Superintendent Blake's desk and seated opposite were Paul and Patricia, who were looking a lot more in control now. We were obviously a bit late in coming into the conversation as Blake read out from the statement he was reading.

'So you arrived about four-thirty pm, the front door was closed but unlocked, you both entered the premises and called out to Detective Sergeant Lambert but there was no answer.' He glanced at the very nervous looking Patsy. 'And you, Ms Purcell, found the body lying in the bath and screamed.'

'Yes, that's right, Superintendent, it was just horrible. Then Paul, Mr Lambert, came in and tried to get her out of the bath. He tried to revive her but she kept slipping back into the bath. We both panicked, I'm afraid.'

'Understandable, Ms Purcell. And you, Mr Lambert, rang triple zero and reported the incident.'

'Yes,' Paul replied. 'It looked like she slipped and fell into the bath and hit her head on the side. I never for a moment thought she could've been murdered. Are you sure?'

'Nothing definite at this stage but we are making inquiries – just routine, you understand. The pathology examination revealed severe bruising around the neck and shoulders consistent with a struggle. You didn't notice it?'

'No, I guess I wasn't paying any attention to that, I was so upset.'

'And you say the front door was unlocked. Was that usual, would you say?'

'I wouldn't think so. In fact I was quite surprised. Lucky was always so careful with her security. When we were living together I was always on to her about being over-cautious with keeping the doors locked. If she was only going to the corner shop she'd lock up. I must say it got to be a bit of a pain in the arse at times. I guess she must've become a bit lax. She would've just got home tired from her shift and must have forgotten.'

'Or somebody had a key? Did you have a key, Mr Lambert?' Blake inquired amiably.

'No. Since we've been separated and Lucky moved into her own place, she didn't want me barging in on her unannounced. That's why I'd rung her earlier that day and told her I'd be dropping in for her to sign some papers regarding the settlement of our divorce.'

That's not true, Lucky whispered to Tony. He never rang me.

'Well, I tried to ring her but she wasn't answering,' Paul said, 'so I took the chance. The station told me her shift would be over at three o'clock.'

Tony looked at me and I shrugged.

'And was it an amicable divorce, Mr Lambert?' Blake continued.

36

'Yes, very amicable,' replied Paul.

'And you can't think of anyone who may have wanted to harm your ex-wife?'

Paul gave the impression of racking his brain and then shook his head.

'No, nobody I can think of. If in fact she was murdered, which I think extremely unlikely, it would more than likely be someone tied in with her work, I would imagine. I'm sure police officers make a lot of enemies. On the other hand, she may have got into a scrape with a felon during the day and sustained the marks on her body then.'

No, it was the bloody killer, stupid, I yelled, ineffectively under the circumstances.

'We'll check that out, of course,' Blake said, making a note on the pad in front of him. 'Any other suspects come to mind? I mean, did she ever discuss her work with you? Any cases she was working on?'

Paul shook his head again.

'We made it a point never to discuss her work.'

That's not quite true, Paul. We did talk about some things apart from *your* work and how much money you were bringing in. I'm sure we occasionally discussed a case I was working on which kept me out late and which gave you the opportunity to get out whoring.

'Anyway,' Paul continued, 'I'm sure you have the files on all her cases going back years. That should show up any likely suspects if there are any.'

'Oh, we'll be checking those, rest assured, Mr Lambert. And you didn't notice anyone suspicious in the vicinity when you arrived? I mean, according to pathology, your ex-wife must have died or been killed only a short time before you arrived.'

Again the shake of the head. 'No.'

Blake stared at Paul for some time and Paul sighed.

'Well, if there's nothing else, I'm afraid I have to get back to work, Superintendent,' he said, rising.

Blake nodded.

'We'll be in touch, Mr Lambert.'

As Paul and Patricia left, I heard Patricia say, 'What an awful man, he made it sound like you were a suspect.'

To which Paul replied, 'I'm the ex-husband. We're always the first suspect. Lucky you were with me when we found her. Otherwise I would've been in deep shit. Anyway, I'm sure they'll find it was an accident.'

Back in Blake's office, a Homicide Detective Sergeant Howell knocked and entered. He was a big man, probably around 190cm, in his mid-forties, unremarkable features, broad shouldered but thickening around the waist. Obviously he needed a few regular sessions in the gym to get him back in to shape; too much desk work and beer. His dark hair had an orange tint to it which was obviously a sign of using one of those men's hair dyes to camouflage the grey. Vanity perhaps? Time for a touch-up, Sarge.

He was wearing civvies: dark brown slacks and a cream, short-sleeved shirt with an open collar which revealed curly grey chest hair. Should have extended the dye job to his chest, I thought.

'What d'you reckon?' Howell asked.

'He seems clean,' Blake replied. 'If he was going to do his wife in I doubt he'd take that blowsy woman with him. She doesn't strike me as the jealous, love-sick, sexually competitive, rival type. His alibi checks out. From what we saw at his office, there were plenty of other contenders for that position, or any other position he fancied, if you ask me, who would fit the bill. He was in the office all day and invited her to accompany him to witness his wife's signature.'

He closed the file in front of him and put it to one side.

'If it was murder, I think it's much more likely to be somebody connected to a case she was or had been working on in the past,' he said. 'You might like to check out her movements for that day and, failing any mention in her report that she'd been attacked during her shift, you could have a look at a possible revenge attack. She could've forgotten to lock the door when she got home so at the moment it looks like an accident. She also could've sustained those marks by falling against the bath and hitting her head.'

'Oh, really?' I said. 'Come on, Tony, we're wasting our time here – back to the office.'

A quick thank you to the guide and in a flash we were back in our Heavenly abode.

I sat at my desk deep in thought trying to work out my next move. Tony now appeared to have set up his work station next to me and was busily typing away at his computer.

'It's no good, Tony,' I said. 'I've got to talk to people and ask questions. Eighty percent of investigation is done by asking questions. How am I supposed to do that when nobody can hear me?'

He shrugged. Obviously he was a newcomer here and hadn't fully worked out the protocol either. Why the hell can't Joseph give me a hand? He's supposed to be my own private guide. Surely he's aware of the facts, who was responsible. Well, he'd been noticeably absent since I arrived at the department. Obviously I've got to work things out for myself. But why? A spiritual exercise, perhaps? How can Blake and the others solve the case where there are absolutely no clues?

Suddenly the conversation with my astral-travelling mother popped into my mind. A psychic? A medium? Would that be possible? Nah, they're not reliable and there are an awful lot of fakes out there. I remember many cases where the police were offered psychic help and the mediums were only out for the publicity and to make a name for themselves and their dodgy profession. Officially, the police regulations forbade accepting evidence from psychics. Ding-bats were always pestering the police claiming to have received spiritual clues and even the names of suspects but it seldom came to anything. All it did was take up valuable police time with little, if any, tangible results. Mostly they were amateur sleuths who deluded themselves that they were in touch with spirits who were directing them to the crime scene and describing suspects, events and locations of missing persons or bodies.

On the other hand, there had been the odd case that was inexplicable and it was even rumoured that a few detectives had secret psychic contacts they used unofficially. Where else can I go? It might be worth investigating. Oh hell, what have I got to lose?

I hit the search engine for 'reliable psychics' and the screen was immediately filled with names. Next to each entry was a star rating system, with a maximum rating of five. I wondered who had gone to the trouble of actually rating them and how. I suppose there was a special software section that was responsible. I decided to only look at three-star rating and above. It didn't appear that there were any five-star ratings at all, which didn't give me a lot of confidence. I idly scrolled through the names and records of success, which was interesting. I noticed Mother's psychic, Magda Vollansky, only rated a one and a half star, which didn't surprise me. Mother was so easily taken in.

I noted down a few of the three-star-rated mediums and decided I'd try and investigate some of them without their knowing if it was possible. Well, if I suddenly appeared in their circle of influence, and if they were any good, certainly they'd be aware of an intruder, wouldn't they? This was all so silly but I had to give it a go. I mean, I had thought there probably wasn't anything after you shuffled off the mortal coil and look at me now.

I talked it over with Tony expecting a well-deserved chiacking but, to my surprise, he took it all seriously and agreed it was worth a try. He offered his help if I needed it but I said I didn't think anything would come of it and I was just investigating it as a possible line of inquiry.

So I set off to the first address, which was a woman called, improbably, Zena. She lived in the hills just outside Hepburn. I remembered it was pretty country around there so it should be a pleasant trip, anyway. I did the old meditate-and-focus trick and, whammy, I was there hovering above a lovely old farmhouse in the foothills. Again, I was intercepted by her guide and protector and I explained the situation. She was a kindly soul who warned me that I might have a bit of trouble with Zena's control who was very possessive and, in her opinion, a bit impatient.

I floated down to the farmhouse and, sure enough, there was her control sitting on the corrugated iron roof, taking in the view I suppose. The farmhouse itself was in poor condition and really needed a coat of paint and some repair work. There was a chimney emitting a curl of grey smoke that disappeared into the pale blue, cloud-studded sky. The garden was somewhat overgrown with untended flower beds that insisted on blooming anyway, as if they had a will of their own. A small vegetable garden out the back appeared to be well looked after with healthy tomatoes, carrots, beans, lettuce and the odd pumpkin. A couple of citrus trees were in fruit and the weeds had been cleared from their trunks. The lawns were cut but the edges untrimmed, creating a ruffle border effect.

I introduced myself to the control and explained what I was trying to do. I discovered her name was Elizabeth – well, that's what she said I could call her – and that the guide had been right: Elizabeth's manner was a little gruff and not all that friendly.

'Well, I *suppose* it will be alright,' she said grudgingly, 'but you're not to make a sound while she's doing the reading. She gets a bit confused even when I'm trying to talk to her so another spirit talking to her at the same time would be chaotic. She's over eighty years old now and pretty deaf so she tends to get my messages a bit mixed up at times. She used to be very good in her younger days but she's gone off the boil in the last ten years or so. I think she'll lose her grading soon. If they give her a one star I'd be surprised.'

I promised not say a thing and just sit in to see if she'd be useful with my investigation.

'I doubt it,' said Elizabeth. 'She can hardly find her way to the bathroom. Wilma has to help her.'

'Wilma?'

'Her guide. I don't do domestic or personal caring duties, that's Wilma's responsibility.'

Oh, so there's a separation of duties even in the spirit world.

'So how does this work, Elizabeth?'

'Well, I'm constantly in tune with my superiors and they tell me what I can pass on and what I can't.'

'Why is that?' I asked.

'Well, there are some things the subjects aren't to know. It might interfere with the path they're on. We're allowed to give them some clues but it's eventually up to them what they do with them. There's no easy, hand it on a plate in the afterlife, you know.'

I was beginning to learn that.

'You're in a bit of luck,' Elizabeth said. 'She's got a reading due any minute now.'

And at that moment, a little yellow Toyota sedan drove up the driveway and parked. A young woman got out, made her way to the front door and tentatively knocked.

'Here we go,' said Elizabeth, and with that she floated down through the roof.

I had a strong feeling that this was going to be one hell of a waste of time but it would give me an idea of what to expect in future visits.

I drifted through the roof and ceiling and hung around up in a corner of the room just as the old lady arrived through the door with the young woman in tow. The medium was very old, grey haired, plump and stooped, and wore an old, purple floral house dress with a matching scarf tied around her head in a twenties sort of style. She invited the young guest to sit at the table opposite, lit a foul-smelling incense stick, took a pack of Tarot cards from a sandalwood box, and unwrapped the cards from a square of black velvet cloth. She tottered back to her seat and sank onto the chair. She closed her eyes and breathed deeply.

'Are you there, Mustafa?'

Mustafa?

Elizabeth answered in a terrible Middle Eastern accent.

'I am here, Zena.'

Elizabeth suddenly appeared at my side and whispered, 'She likes a bit of the exotic.'

'Can you hear me, Mustafa?' Zena intoned dramatically.

'Yes, I can, Zena.'

'Right,' said Zena, as she placed the pack of cards in front of the young woman. 'Now shuffle the cards and place them in front of me.'

The young woman's hands shook a little as she picked up the cards and shuffled. Unfortunately, in her agitated state, she shuffled the cards a little too vigorously and they popped out of her hands and scattered all over the floor.

43

'Oops, sorry,' said the young woman as she jumped to her feet to retrieve the cards.

'No, don't touch them,' Zena ordered. 'I'll get them.'

Zena painfully rose from her chair, shuffled around the table, wheezing with every breath and stooped to gather the cards. She then wobbled back to her chair. Placing the cards in front of the young woman she instructed her to lay them out in a particular pattern. Still apologising for her carelessness, which Zena waved away dismissively, the young woman did as she was instructed.

'You have before you a lady with the initials J S,' said Elizabeth.

'Your initials are J S?' Zena said to the young woman.

The young woman nodded.

'Jean Sutter – I told you that on the phone. I wanted to ask you about my boyfriend.'

'Jean Sutter, that's right,' said Zena. 'Do you have any messages about her boyfriend for her, Mustafa?'

'His initials are R for Robert.'

Zena repeated this and Jean nodded.

'He works as a student veterinarian. He's very good and he'll go far,' said Elizabeth.

'He's a prudent vegetarian but he's moving away,' said Zena.

'Oh,' said Jean disappointedly.

'No, he's a vet and he'll do well in his job!' Elizabeth repeated.

'But he'll do well wherever he goes,' Zena said quickly.

'But where will he be moving to?' asked Jean.

'Tell her he'll be getting a job at the Zoo.'

'He's going to Peru.'

Jean looked astounded.

'No, the Zoo! In Melbourne!' Elizabeth enunciated clearly.

'Well, somewhere where there's a lot of big animals,' Zena flustered.

'But he'll send for her and they'll get married,' Elizabeth said, 'and they'll be very happy and successful.'

'But everything will work out,' said Zena. 'You'll be a lovely bride. You'll wear a beautiful cream lace dress and carry pink roses and live in a lovely big house in Melbourne. I see three children, two boys and a girl. The girl will be a good student but the boys will be plodders. But they'll get there if they apply themselves. Your mother hasn't been well ...'

'She died last year,' Jean said sadly.

'Yes, she wasn't well at all,' said Zena, 'but she's in a better place now, dear. She sends her love and will always watch over you.'

'Don't get carried away, Zena,' Elizabeth sighed warningly. 'Just listen to me carefully.'

But Zena was off on a roll, predicting a small win in the lottery, a chest infection for Robert for which she recommended prayer and natural remedies, a stranger entering her father's life and an old friend to reappear and possibly cause trouble.

I'm outta here.

I thanked Elizabeth and told her I had other calls to make and I was gone in a flash.

Chapter 5

The next contender lived in the Dandenong Ranges, in a neat, modern little house with a trellis of yellow roses over the front door. The control was calling himself Alf, and claimed to be an ex-waterside worker. He was a roly-poly, middle-aged man in shorts and a navy blue Jackie Howe singlet. I explained my mission and he looked very doubtful.

'Ah, I dunno,' he said. 'Penelope's a bit of a prude; very religious and gets the hot flushes whenever she has to deal with sex or violence. Lovely woman but a bit straight laced for her own good. She's usually right on the button when it comes to predictions, though. But she translates the messages to suit herself. Hang on a tick, she's in the middle of a reading now and she's just asked me a question. What was that, Penelope?'

'I said, Mrs Blacksmith was asking about her husband.'

Penelope was certainly a straight-laced-looking person, even severe; thin as a rail, prune faced really, dressed completely in black in a straight, shapeless, ankle-length dress, black, flat-heeled court shoes, her black hair, streaked with grey, pulled back severely into a knot. At her throat she wore a fine gold crucifix.

On the wall behind her were several paintings of Jesus looking rather pained and downright uncomfortable on the cross and one displaying him with a bleeding heart. At least the one with the bleeding heart looked a bit more cheerful.

'Oh, yeah,' Alf said, 'her husband karked it a few months ago, heart condition. He was shagging her best friend and his heart gave out just as he was working up to the final thrust. Talk about coitis interruptis. The lady friend was very pissed off. She threw her clothes on and skedaddled out of his bedroom and out the front door, without a by your leave. The missus came home only a few minutes later from her afternoon at the bowls club, perfect timing. She lost a packet, I might add. She found him dead on the bed in their room. She called the ambulance but it was too late. By then, he was shooting down the tunnel towards the light on a one-way ticket.'

There was a long pause while Penelope absorbed this and her mouth tightened to the size of a current.

'I see your poor late husband dying of a massive heart attack. It was very sudden and quick. He didn't suffer, I can assure you. Up until that moment he'd been very happy, exercising a little too strenuously. He should have taken precautions but from what I can see, obviously he didn't. In some ways that was a good thing, to find him like that. He looked so contented and peaceful.'

'That's exactly how it happened, Penelope, you are amazing!' said Mrs Blacksmith in awe.

'And I think you were out at a sporting venue at the time. Not really enjoying yourself because your friend, Margaret, couldn't be with you. She was occupied in one of her favourite hobbies that she shared an interest in with your dear husband, Jeff.'

'That's right! They were in a Scrabble competition earlier that day!'

'Yes, well, she'll have to find another partner now, I'm afraid. I think she's looking at another friend's husband – Trevor?'

'Oh, that will be Sandra's husband, he's very active and competitive.'

'Yes, well, she should keep a close eye on him. His heart is also a bit weak. He could fall into the same trap as your husband.'

'I'll mention it to her.'

47

'Yes, I suggest you tell her that the strain might be too much for both of them.'

'And what about young Leisel?' asked Mrs Blacksmith.'

'She's her daughter,' said Alf. 'A right little whore, having it off all over the place. Raves, dance parties, you name it. Also into the party drugs and booze. If she doesn't pull herself together and get rid of that boyfriend, Greg, she'll end up pregnant and in rehab.'

'She's a very active young lady, isn't she?' Penelope said to Mrs Blacksmith. 'Loves a good time, very … spirited. There's a young man she's involved with, a … Greg? Well, he isn't the best influence on her, I'm afraid. Someone should warn her off him. There could be unhappy consequences.'

'I've told her that,' said Mrs Blacksmith, 'but you know these young people, you can't tell them anything. And my boy, Gerald, any messages for him?'

'He's as gay as a sparrow,' Alf said. 'He and his mate, Simon, have been having it off since high school. Nice couple though. They're going to open a women's fashion business. Gerald will do the designing and Simon will handle the business side. They'll make a bloody fortune. When the Government ever get around to equality in the marriage act, those two will be one of the first couples mincing down the aisle.'

Penelope's mouth was now stringlike as she replied.

'He's such a sensitive boy,' she translated, 'very artistic. I see he's into design and I also see him and a friend going into business. They'll do very well. Ah, I also see a wedding in the future.'

'Oh,' said Mrs Blacksmith, thrilled, 'what's she like?'

'Different,' replied Penelope. 'I think you'll be rather surprised. But they'll be very happy.'

After the reading finished, Alf said, 'Well, what did ya think?'

'Well, she's obviously very good,' I replied, 'but I think I'd rather have somebody who told it more as it is, a little more straightforward.'

'Yeah, I see what you mean,' said Alf. 'She does dress it up a bit.'

A bit? I thought. She smoothes it on with a trowel! I want somebody on the same wavelength as me.

So, on to the last one on my list for this excursion. I was beginning to have serious doubts about the whole idea. As it happened, the next candidate just happened to live in St Kilda, not far from the Police Station, so I thought I'd drop in and see if Blake had come up with any more information after I'd checked out the next psychotic psychic chick.

I hovered over the address and immediately noticed something was very different. It was a small block of four apartments. Evelyn, the psychic, apparently lived in one of the ground-floor units, which opened up at the back onto a small, enclosed courtyard crowded with herbs and flowering pot plants of all shapes and sizes. A mass of terracotta wall plaques decorated the brick walls and a small outdoor furniture setting and recliner completed the décor. On one side of the courtyard stood a single garage, which provided privacy from the next door unit, all very suburban and normal.

The first thing I noticed that was different was that I hadn't encountered any guide or control keeping guard. I sensed what I could only describe as a presence and shadowy, discarnate entities flitting about but none approached me. I also noticed a sort of thin, shining, blue ray of light shooting up into the sky through the roof of the apartment block. Strange, I thought.

I drifted down and saw Evelyn pottering about with the plants. She was a voluptuous woman in her late fifties or early sixties, of medium height, wearing a colourful silk caftan in bright autumn colours and a funny, red, knitted, brimless headcap, which she obviously wore to hide her thinning grey hair. Her face had once been pretty but age had lined the once-pale fine skin and thickened her arms, neck and chins.

I settled onto the recliner and watched her as she bent and loosened the soil, weeded and watered the pots. I saw her back tense for a second but she continued with her gardening. After a time, without standing or turning, she said, 'Piss off.'

For a moment I thought she was talking to a grub that had dared attack her plants but as there was no response she turned her head directly towards me and repeated her greeting.

'I said, piss off.'

'Hi,' I said brightly,' I'm Lucky.'

'No you're not,' she said. 'I'm no longer in the business.'

'No,' I laughed, 'my name's Lucielle, I'm nicknamed Lucky.'

'I'm still not in the business,' she replied and turned back to her pots.

'But you've got a three-star rating on the Akashic Web.'

'Three star? Is that all?' She seemed a mite put out. 'What happened to the fourth one?'

I shrugged.

'Probably because I stopped practising,' she muttered.

'And why would you do that? You're obviously very good.'

She turned and eyeballed me, accusingly.

'Do you know what it's like seeing dead people all the time? It's exhausting and it gets very upsetting sometimes. I've been seeing dead people for as long as I can remember and I just got to the stage where I said, okay, enough is enough.'

'Yeah, I know what you mean. It must be a bit of a drag — emotionally, I mean. I wouldn't have bothered you but,' I paused for effect, 'I have a problem and I think only a genuine, talented psychic can help me. You see, I was a cop and I was murdered.'

50

'Big guy, dressed in black, balaclava, tattoos,' she interrupted automatically.

'Yes! Exactly! You know him?'

'I'm a psychic not a bikie's moll,' she replied dryly.

'He's a bikie?' I asked, amazed.

'Well, he rides a motor bike, I just saw him.'

'Where?'

'I had one of those bloody flashbacks,' she said, seemingly disgusted with herself.

'And?' I prompted.

'And nothing. I just got a quick glimpse. Go on.'

'Well, when I arrived up there,' I indicated the Heavens, 'or wherever it is, I was transferred into their CIA, that's the Celestial Investigation Agency, and told I had to solve the case myself – part of my development course, or something. Well, to solve the case, I have to interview people and they can't hear or see me! So I thought if I could find a really genuine, talented psychic,' I repeated, hoping I wasn't laying it on too thick, 'she might be able to help me out.'

'And how would this genuine, talented psychic do that?'

'Well, you see, I thought she might get an insight, and if she could ask the questions and let me know the answers, it might help me figure out who attacked me.'

'Well, that's a different sort of sob story. Wouldn't they help you out up there?' she copied my gesture to the Heavens.

I shook my head.

'But they know everything up there,' she said. 'They have access to any information they want. They could put you straight on to the killer.'

I shrugged.

'Well, there must be a reason,' she said thoughtfully, 'there always is. Obviously you have a lesson to learn and this is part of the test.'

'Maybe you're part of the test too,' I suggested helpfully, hoping I wasn't pushing my luck too far. 'Maybe I was supposed to find you and maybe bring you back into the fold, so to speak.'

She shook her head, determinedly. 'No way. I'm happy to let the dead rest in peace, thank you. I'm sick of ghosts cluttering up my apartment and my life. '

'I'm not a ghost. I like to think of myself as a free spirit.'

Evelyn laughed coarsely.

'Honey, you is what you is and believe me, I've had the experience to know what you is.'

'Well, will you at least think about it? I promise I won't get in your way. I'd just feed you the names of the people I want questioned and what to ask them. I wouldn't put you in any danger.'

She looked at me shrewdly for a long time, weighing up the possible consequences.

'Tell you what, I'll think about it and let you know.'

'But how will you do that?'

She thought for a moment and then inspiration hit her.

'We'll have a password. When you hear it, you'll know to come running, or rather flying.'

I gave her my brightest smile.

'Oh, thanks, Evelyn, you're a doll.'

'I haven't agreed yet,' she reprimanded me. 'I said I'd think about it.'

'Right,' I replied. 'What password will we use?'

She thought for a minute, glancing around the courtyard. Her eyes fell on a terracotta wall plaque with the figure of a four-armed man sitting in the lotus position, which stood out in relief against a background of large leaves and lotus blossoms. It was very Hindu and very beautiful.

'Shiva,' she said. 'God of the yogis. Self-controlled and celibate, which seems appropriate to me as we're both not

52

getting any, that's for sure. He also represents death and destruction of the ego and makes way for a new beginning. He makes us see reality more clearly.'

'Right,' I said. 'Shiva it is.' To get her onside I would have accepted Geronimo. 'But how will I know when you make up your mind?'

'Don't worry, you'll hear me, wherever you are.'

'Right,' I said. 'Shiva – that sounds good to me.'

'Now piss off and let me get back to my gardening.'

'Oh, right. Thanks, Evelyn, it was great talking with you. I hope I hear from you soon. I think we could really work well as a team.'

'Which part of piss off don't you understand?'

'Right,' I said. 'I'll be off then.'

I zapped out of there before I wore out my welcome and hovered back over the police station. I got the okay from the Senior Detective Sergeant guide who simply waved me on and once again I was in Blake's office. He was in the middle of a conversation with Sergeant Howell.

'And,' said Howell, 'according to Lambert's report she didn't encounter any trouble with felons on her last shift so she didn't get those welts from a perp. But, as you said, she could've got them as she fell into the bath.'

'And you say Paul Lambert's lady friend,' Blake said as he checked the file in front of him, 'Patricia Purcell, rang and said she reckons they saw a bloke on a motor cycle as they were leaving the premises? Any description?'

'Not really,' Howell replied. 'The usual, dressed in black leather and a helmet and goggles. She said he almost ran into them as they turned into Lucky's street. He raised a hand to Paul Lambert in apology, apparently, and Lambert acknowledged it. Probably nothing in it.'

53

'But Lambert didn't mention it when we questioned them,' Blake said. 'I asked him if he'd seen anyone suspicious in the neighbourhood and he said no. You'd think he might remember a near miss with a motorcycle.'

'It wasn't Paul,' I shouted. 'It was a big guy with tats wearing a balaclava!' But of course they couldn't hear me. 'It was Paul and that Purcell woman that found me!'

'Keep looking into her current and past cases,' Blake said to Howell. 'There might be someone who bore her a grudge.'

'Well, she was pretty tied up with a drug investigation but didn't seem to be getting anywhere.' Howell suddenly snapped his fingers. 'Just a minute, there was a case she was involved in a few years ago, a domestic – the husband was a bikie. He was sent down for five years. I wonder if he's out yet. I'll check.'

Hmm, I thought, good thinking. That's the one Tony was talking about. I remember that case. But why should I be targeted because of an arrest we made for a simple domestic? We made dozens of arrests for domestics but no one tried to kill us for it. Doesn't make sense. Still, you've got to follow every lead no matter how doubtful it looks. I'd better get back to the office.

The next second I was sitting at my desk.

'Hey, Tony,' I said, 'that domestic you talked about that we worked on, what have we got on it?'

'It's in the file, hang on.'

He hit a couple of keys and read from the screen.

'Scott Warner, 37 Kent Street, Broadmeadows, age twenty-eight, occupation, courier, member of the Rusty Pistons Motor Cycle Club, married to Lucy Warner, no kids, sentenced to five years Fulham Correctional Centre, January 2009.'

He mumbled on and I tuned out. Obviously Warner was still in prison.

I was suddenly aware of a great feeling of love being directed toward me. I turned and there was my darling father standing there, smiling at me.

'Dad!' I screamed in delight as I literally flew into his arms. He felt so good. It was like a fusion of love. I felt him pat my back just as he used to do and I drew back and looked at his oh so familiar face.

'Dad, how wonderful to see you again! I've missed you so much.'

'Hi, kiddo,' he said, still smiling. 'How ya doin'?'

'I'm fine, just fine,' I said and I swear I was choking up with tears of happiness. 'So, you actually made it up here? And you always said you'd probably go straight to Hell,' I said jokingly.

'They kicked me out of Hell. They said I was too much damn trouble,' he replied laughingly. 'Besides, I had a job to do.'

'What was that?'

'Looking after your mother,' he replied. 'Mind you, that's a sort of Hell in itself.'

'Oh, Dad, you poor thing, how can you stand it?'

'I guess because I love her,' he said simply. 'I always have and I guess I always will.'

I looked at him, doubtfully.

'You don't understand, kiddo, you didn't know her when we were young. She was a very vulnerable, beautiful person. She still is. She lost her mother and father to illness when she was only fourteen years old; an age when you really need your parents' influence and love. They died within a few months of each other. She didn't know who she was; she felt abandoned. She covers up that loss with all that social crap because it gives her an identity. But we have a lot of history together. Not just in the last life but many times before.'

He paused, and I was about to ask him what he'd been doing since he arrived but he continued, 'I got very sick just after you

55

were born. They thought I wasn't going to make it. She looked after me like you wouldn't believe. She took over the running of the business to support us; she nursed me while she was looking after you as a baby. She was very frightened yet he never showed it or complained. And you never knew, how could you?'

He smiled. 'Do you remember your first day at school? You were so little. When she came home from dropping you off, she didn't know that I heard her but she collapsed into a flood of tears. She hated leaving you alone there but she knew she had to. She wouldn't send you to after-school care or day care for any reason. She'd take you into the office and sit you on a chair or on the floor with books and toys while she worked.'

More flashes came of me sitting on the floor in my mother's office, playing with coloured pencils and paper. I suddenly felt very guilty and flashes from the past continued to run riot in my memories. But Joseph's voice came into my head.

'You weren't to know, she blocked you out. You were only a child. You couldn't understand why she couldn't return your love.'

I looked around and there was Joseph, dressed in a Police Superintendent's uniform! He nodded and smiled. I sort of smiled back in recognition but then he was gone.

'When I eventually recovered,' Dad went on, 'and I was able to take up the reins again, she still held onto the fear that she'd lose us and covered it up with the attitude that she didn't really care. She was haunted by the fear of loss. But I saw the old terrified look come back into her eyes every time one of us had even a sniffle. So you see, kiddo, that's why I look over her, love and history.'

Feeling somewhat awkward and, I must admit, a little confused, I changed the subject and we chattered about fond memories of our time together on the earthly plane; memories we shared of companionship and love, which seemed to play out in a film version we could both appreciate. The interesting thing was that, although we had visited many exotic places around the world in our earthly travels, the actual locations were not that important. The things that affected us most were the feelings, the emotions we shared, both positive and negative.

We were just sharing an experience we'd had on a short trip to Egypt where we'd visited the Cairo Museum and the Pyramids and the Luxor and Karnak temples and the feelings they engendered, when Dad suddenly said, 'Oops, she's about to wake. I'd better get down there and try to jolly her up. She has terrible mornings.'

With that he was gone.

I went to continue my investigation on the web but a blast of sound vibrated in my being and almost shattered my composure.

'Shiva! Get your pert little arse down here!'

Obviously it was Evelyn.

Chapter 6

She was in her kitchenette adjoining her living room, making herself a cup of coffee. A plate of chocolate biscuits sat on the table ready for eager consumption. As soon as she sensed I'd arrived, she spun around to face me.

'We've gotta get another call sign,' she said, firmly. 'The moment I called you, I was inundated with a pack of Indian Hindu spirits flitting all over the place. I didn't think; Shiva is a very popular name for boys in India. They came running!'

I stifled a laugh, imagining the apartment swamped with little brown Hindu entities and Evelyn abusing them and sending them packing.

'How about I just call, "Evelyn here"?'

'You mean you've decided to help me?' I asked hopefully.

'Ah, I might as well,' she said reluctantly. 'It's a bit different to reassuring dead people and pointing them to the Light. I always fancied myself as an undercover cop. Besides, it might stand me in good stead when it's my time to go. And I think it was rotten what happened to you and I think they should be giving you a bit more help.'

I floated up close to her and placed my hand on her arm.

'Thanks, Evelyn, I know that decision was hard.'

She attempted to brush my hand away but of course that didn't work so she moved away a few steps and turned back to me, coffee cup in hand.

'Now, what do you want me to do?'

'Well, for a start, I picked up a bit of information at the station after I left you. They had a phone call from the woman who was with Paul when they found me. She'd remembered that they almost had a run-in with a guy on a motorcycle as they were turning into my street. Of course it may just be a coincidence but when I checked some of my old cases, I came across a file on a domestic where we'd arrested the husband who was a member of a motor cycle club called the Rusty Pistons.'

'The Rusty Piss Tins?' Evelyn asked incredulously, spluttering and almost choking on her coffee and spitting bits of chocolate biscuits everywhere.

'Don't go there, Evelyn, I've already done that one. No, p-i-s-t-o-n-s, like in an engine.'

'Ah!' she said, recovering somewhat. 'So you'd like me to see if there could be a connection? What was this bloke's name?'

'Scott Warner. But it couldn't be him because he's serving five years in prison for grievous bodily harm and drug trafficking. But maybe it could be a revenge killing by one of his mates. Another strange thing I remembered was that the young constable who was my partner on that day was spending his day off fishing alone and he supposedly fell and hit his head on a rock and drowned in the river.'

Her eyebrows raised and the corners of her mouth turned down.

'Bit of a coincidence – hit on the head and drowned? How do you know that?'

'He told me.'

'How could he tell you if he's dead?'

She suddenly realised who she was talking to.

'Oh.'

'We met up on the other side of the white light,' I explained. 'In fact, we're sort of partners again. He's working with me on my case. Really nice guy and quite a hunk, if I remember correctly.'

'I don't suppose I'll get to meet him? It's been a long drought.'

'I don't think you want a dead date, do you?'

'I've been on a few of those I can tell you but no, they weren't deceased. Although it was hard to tell sometimes. Now this bikie guy, Warner, do you have an address?'

'He lived at 37 Kent Street, Broadmeadows, but I don't know where the motorcycle club's headquarters are.'

'Probably in the vicinity. There'd be a pub they'd frequent nearby, I imagine. I'll check it out.'

'That'd be a great help. But Broadmeadows is a long way away, have you got wheels?'

She drew herself up proudly with a superior sneer.

'I am the proud owner of a bright red, vintage, 1977, Paggio Vespa PX motor scooter, in mint condition I might add. I have a friend who's a fantastic mechanic and a huge fan of vintage scooters and bikes. He's modified it and brought it up to the latest specifications. And even better, he's cheap.'

'But the fuel costs – I can't recompense you. I don't think my fuel allowance is current anymore.'

'Not to worry, she runs on the smell of an oily rag – 60 to 70 mpg. And it will give me an excuse for a bit of a run.'

A flash of this strange, wonderful, plump, ageing lady, astride a vintage motor scooter, putt-putting through the city at ten kilometres an hour was a bit of a giggle but my heart warmed to her immediately.

'She's got a top speed of eighty ks,' she informed me proudly.'

'Wow! That fast?'

'Only on the open road, of course. And downhill. With a tail wind,' she added. 'But she gets me there.'

She jotted down the address I'd given her on a notepad. 'I'll call you later. Remember, "Evelyn here",' she added.

Seeing I was sort of in the neighbourhood anyway, I thought I might take a quick hover over Mum's house to see if she was okay. I might even bump into Dad and see them both together. I seemed to be drawn there. I didn't enter the house but floated overhead and I could see my mother sitting alone on the couch in the darkened living room, illuminated only by a single table lamp. In her lap she held a photograph album. It was open at the last two pages. On each page was a photograph, one of Dad and one of me in my police uniform. She sat silently, running her finger delicately over the photographs, tears streaming down her face. I felt such compassion for her and yes, love, I realised. What a shame we'd wasted all those years drifting further and further apart.

I was suddenly aware of my father's presence and saw his spirit slowly drift to my mother's side. He put his arms around her shoulders and bent his head to hers. I felt myself unconsciously projecting love and comfort towards them. After a moving moment, she seemed to rally. She slowly closed the album and laid it gently on the side table, no doubt always having it handy for when she felt the need.

Back at my desk, Tony appeared next to me. It was really disconcerting how these people would suddenly appear and disappear, but I was getting used to it.

'Well, you were a busy little copper, weren't you?'

'I did my bit, I suppose, why?'

'I've been checking over your record files more closely and I was pretty amazed at some of your accomplishments. I'm very impressed.'

'Why, thank you sir,' I replied, with what I was sure was a blush.

'Bank robberies, gang wars, kidnappings, a liquor store robbery, knife attacks, shootings, the odd gangland murder, drugs – you've had a hand in them all.'

'That was just on weekdays,' I said, dismissively. 'The weekends were when it really heated up.'

'The more I read, the more I realised how open you were to a revenge attack.'

'Really?' I said amazed. 'How many?'

'Dozens,' he replied.

'Oh, well, I suppose we'd better make a record and follow them through, eh?'

'This could take some time,' he said.

'Time we've got plenty of,' I replied ruefully.

He scrolled down the screen, stopping occasionally to check on what was listed and the details.

'Here's one: a murder. A wife shot her husband because he used to grind his teeth, fart and snore constantly in his sleep.'

'That was a justifiable homicide. Besides, she was a skinny little old lady who'd been married to him for forty years. Any revenge she was after was aimed at him not the arresting officer. Anyway, she died in prison the year after.'

'Oh, yes, I see that now, over in the far column.'

'Keep checking but also look in the results column. We want someone who could logically blame me for causing their downfall; preferably, someone who isn't dead or in prison.'

'How about this one? Two brothers, identical twins, Rex and Reginald Copeland, both arrested for armed robbery, different locations, but the offences happened at exactly the same time on the same day. Both wore matching masks and gloves. Both convenience stores but one made the mistake of shooting the owner of the one he held up. The owner wasn't happy about being robbed for the fourth time and went for the robber with a baseball bat. He died of the gunshot wound in hospital so there was no one to identify the perp. Hmm, tricky.'

'I remember that one,' I said. 'We brought both brothers in on suspicion. They had previous. You couldn't really tell them apart. Confusion was their MO. We also brought in the other shop owner but he never saw his robber's face but he confirmed it was the same sort of mask. They were vampire masks.'

'So how did you solve the case?'

'We didn't, not entirely. The brothers were playing it smart. They blamed each other for the shooting but they were different offences and different penalties so consequently we had to find out which was which. We had to find out which one was the shooter and which one was the thief. As you say, it was a tricky one.'

'How did you finally tell them apart?'

'We couldn't so they both went down for armed robbery but we couldn't pin the murder on either of them. They were furious that their subterfuge was discovered. They'd covered up for each other for years, one acting as an alibi for the other, but by doing both robberies at the same time in the same outfits, neither had an alibi. I swore to both of them I'd eventually find out which was the killer and he'd go down for it.'

'A good reason for revenge.'

'But they were common thieves, punks.'

'Would either or both of them be out yet?'

I checked the dates on the file.

'Yep, they're both out roaming the streets again by now.'

'Could be worth checking on,' said Tony.

I shrugged. 'Doubtful, but go for your life.'

'Or yours,' said Tony.

Evelyn was all set to infiltrate the Rusty Pistons Motor Cycle Club. She'd donned a shoulder-length, wavy red wig and dressed herself appropriately, or so she thought, in tight black leather pants, tight black sweatshirt and black helmet. A black leather jacket completed the ensemble. Her makeup was a little on the garish side with bright red lipstick, a smudge too much blush, smoky-grey eye shadow highlighted in purple, and heavy mascara on her eyelashes. Around her neck she wore a chunky gold chain and medallion. On the whole, she looked like a humpback whale searching for a near-sighted mate.

She climbed aboard her trusty vintage Vespa motor scooter and with an ineffectual splutter, puttered out of the garage and down the street heading for adventure. Ignoring angry horn blasts from frustrated drivers, she maintained a steady if rather sedate pace in the outside lane enroute for her destination.

To get her bearings, she decided to make straight for the address in Kent Street, Broadmeadows, that Lucky had given her, and check out the area for a pub that might turn out to be the regular watering hole for the Rusty Pistons Club. However, when she reached the intersection, her way was barred by crime scene tape and several police cars and an ambulance. A crowd had gathered on the corner to gawk at the action so Evelyn pulled into the gutter and parked. Sure enough, the action was centred around number 37. She dismounted and made her way to the edge of the crowd.

'What's going on?' she asked one of the bystanders, an elderly lady in a floral house dress and a lavender cardigan.

'Apparently the nice young lady in 37 drowned herself in the bath, poor thing. Dangerous things, baths. I keep out of them. Such a shame, she was a nice young thing too. Lucy her name was. I think her beast of a husband was due home from prison today, too.'

'Beast, why do say he's a beast?'

'Used to knock her around something awful. It's been lovely and quiet since he was away, too.'

She turned to the woman next to her and whispered, 'I wonder if it was suicide? I mean, with her mongrel husband coming home and all.'

'Wouldn't surprise me in the least,' the other woman whispered back with a knowing sneer. 'He was a nasty piece.'

'What was his name?' Evelyn asked.

'Warner, Scott Warner,' both women chorused back.

The body, swathed in a body bag, was carried out and deposited in the ambulance. The bystanders whispered and pointed a lot.

'Who found her?' asked Evelyn.

'Her next-door neighbour. She called in to deliver a sponge she'd made for the husband's homecoming. I would've laced it with cyanide, the bastard. The front door was open so she went straight in and found her. You could hear the scream miles away. That's her sitting on the gutter with the ambulance attendant and the copper. She's in a right state.'

Evelyn returned to her scooter and in her mind she called, 'Evelyn here! Think you'd better get down to Scott Warner's address. Guess what? His wife's just been found drowned in the bath. He was due out of prison today. Suspected suicide. Sound familiar?'

The message was received loud and clear and I turned to Tony.

'Scott Warner's wife's been found drowned in the bath. He was supposed to get out of prison today. See if you can confirm that. I think I'll take a little jaunt over there and have a look around.'

'Right,' said Tony.

As usual the trip was almost instantaneous and I drifted past the cops and the crime scene tape and into the house. Everything looked normal. An attempt had been made to tidy up with even a welcoming vase of fresh flowers on the kitchen table. The forensics team were at work dusting the place for fingerprints and clues but it looked pretty clean. The body was gone, of course, but I doubt that mattered. I drifted out to see if I could overhear any conversation from the D's. An officer was returning from the patrol car where he'd been on the radio to headquarters. He walked up to the officer in charge.

'Scott Warner was released from prison ten days ago. He was supposed to be returning straight home, here. No one's sighted him since he got out.'

'Uh huh,' said the OIC. 'Put out an APB on him. I think we should have a chat.'

Chapter 7

Evelyn found a local pub that looked a likely possibility. It was called Stan's Tavern and there were several motor bikes parked outside. She entered the pub giving her rendition of a sexy swagger as she walked over to the bar, removing her helmet as she went.

The barmaid set down a tray of glasses she had just removed from the dishwasher on the counter behind the bar.

'What'll it be, luv?'

To her credit she didn't drop the glasses in shock on seeing the apparition before her.

'A half vodka, lime and lemonade, thanks,' said Evelyn. 'I'm driving.'

As the barmaid poured, Evelyn glanced around the room noting a few biker types sitting on stools and a couple playing pool.

'This wouldn't be the hangout for the Rusty Pistons, would it?'

'Sure is, luv, that's a couple of the guys over there.' The barmaid indicated the pool players.

'Where's their clubhouse?'

'About a block down this road – can't miss it, big yellow garage.' She took in Evelyn's attire and gave a quirky smile. 'Why, thinking of becoming a member?'

'Maybe. Just thought I'd check it out.'

'They're proper ravers that lot, luv. Better watch yourself.'

'I can handle m'self,' Evelyn said, straightening up to her full 158 centimetres, squaring her shoulders and trying to look as tough as her appearance allowed. She downed her drink in one gulp and pushed the money across the counter.

'Keep the change, sweetheart,' she said as she turned and made her way to the exit.

'Wow, a whole ten cents!' the barmaid cried. The couple of drinkers on the stools collapsed in laughter.

Evelyn donned her helmet, mounted her scooter and took off down the street in the direction the barmaid had indicated. Sure enough, about a block later, Evelyn saw the building the barmaid had described: bright yellow with faded red trim, two storey, double-fronted with half of the street frontage taken up by what looked like a workshop, with large open doors revealing tools, parts and motor bikes in various stages of repair. A petrol pump stood to one side and more bikes were parked outside.

Evelyn parked, dismounted and took off her helmet letting the red, wavy tresses of her wig cascade over her shoulders. Shaking the locks in what she thought of as a provocative way, she slipped her leather jacket off, casually threw it over her shoulder and approached the workshop. She was aware of two tough-looking characters in greasy jeans and T-shirts watching her. They were in their late twenties or early thirties, she estimated, rather cute in a rough trade sort of way and well muscled, she could tell, by the bulging T-shirts and tight sleeves. She did appreciate a bit of blue-collar, butch masculinity.

'Hi, darlin',' one of them said as she approached. 'Your wheels?'

'Sure are. Paggio Vespa 150cc,' she said proudly.

'Yeah, it looks like a 1977 model, single cylinder, two-stroke, but I'd say it's had a few modifications, by the look of it. Twelve-inch alloy wheels and I bet it's got front and rear disc brakes.'

Evelyn nodded. 'Now it's got a four-stroke, automatic transmission gearbox with a 278cc capacity. Brought it up to a GTS 300 model. You know your bikes.'

The young man smirked as he glanced at his mate.

'Oh, yeah, I know an old bike when I see one.'

His mate laughed coarsely.

'What can I do for ya, luv, you want a re-bore?'

Evelyn gave her most provocative smile.

'If you've got the time, big boy.'

The men exchanged looks and as one they said, 'No,' and returned to their work.

Evelyn ignored the insult.

'Actually, I was looking for the Rusty Pistons Club,' she said with all the dignity she could muster.

'You've come to the right place.' The young man didn't look up from his work.

'I've just come up from Tasmania,' she said, 'and I was thinking of joining a club up here. What do I have to do to join?'

'Next door, luv.' He flicked a gesture towards the other end of the building. 'Fill out the application form and pay ya dues and Bob's ya uncle. Or maybe ya next boyfriend.' He sniggered, that was the only word for it. 'You'll have to be passed by the committee, though.'

'Oh,' she said somewhat surprised, 'is that all?'

'Yep,' he said, still without looking up.

The conversation had obviously come to its natural conclusion so she thanked them and wandered back out and along the building where she found a door with a sign reading, Rusty Pistons Motor Cycle Club, Members Only. She removed her helmet, tucked it under one arm, opened the door and entered.

Evelyn stopped in surprise at the sight before her. She'd expected a rundown hovel smelling of beer and probably marijuana, with a few wobbly tables and chairs and maybe a couple of threadbare couches and posters of motorbikes and naked women adorning the wall. But instead she was confronted by a very clean and tidy, spacious room, painted cream and decorated in complimentary autumn tones. It was furnished with tasteful vinyl and laminated tables and chairs, cream couches and armchairs, bookshelves stacked with books and magazines depicting motor bikes on their covers, curtained windows and framed posters of members enjoying days out in the country or beside the beach. It was a very warm and welcoming place.

But what really shocked her were the twenty or so inhabitants. There didn't appear to be one who was under sixty years of age! She was also aware of a number of Earth-bound souls hanging around looking rather sad. Must have been ex-members who were drawn back to the place where they'd been happy with their friends and couldn't or wouldn't let go. But right then she didn't have the time or the inclination to instruct them on how to move on or advance to the next stage because she had other priorities.

The live members were all dressed in clean, bright casual wear, slacks, shirts or blouses and boots. Hooks and hatstands held riding jackets, goggles and helmets. The riding jackets all had the Rusty Pistons logo on the back, a silver piston on a dark green background with the club name emblazoned in red underneath. As she stood in the entrance the happy chatter in the room came to an abrupt stop with every eye turning in her direction.

After an embarrassed pause, she smiled a little over-brightly.
'Hi, I'm Pixie.'
Another awkward pause followed until a middle-aged blonde woman, wearing a rather smart brown outfit with an orange floral silk scarf hanging loosely around her neck, rose from one

of the armchairs, smiled brightly and approached her with extended hand.

'Hello, Pixie, I'm Valerie. I'm the president of the Rusty Pistons. Can I help you?'

'Well, I don't know,' Evelyn stuttered. 'I mean, I was hoping to join a club, a motorcycle club, but this isn't …' She stumbled to a stop.

'… what you expected?' Valerie finished the sentence for her with a smile. 'You were expecting a rough, uncouth crowd with hairy arms and chests?'

The rest of the members roared with laughter.

'Well, there's always Maureen,' one of the old blokes yelled out, which was met with another roar of laughter.

'You were expecting us to be OMGs or One Percenters?'

Evelyn looked uncertain as to what Valerie was talking about.

'OMGs? – Oh My Gods?'

Valerie laughed as did most of the rest of the members.

'OMGs, Outlaw Motor Gangs,' Valerie explained. 'Or OMC's, Outlaw Motor Clubs. Only about one percent of motor cycle clubs are outlawed, so hence the term One Percenters.'

'Oh. Really,' Evelyn responded, uncertainly. 'Well, you learn something new every day, don't you?'

'We're an over-fifties club, as you can see. It's a sort of social club where the members all have an interest in riding. We hold rallies and trips away, barbeques, social gatherings with other clubs, you name it. It's great fun. Come and meet some of the others.'

She took Evelyn's arm and led her around the room introducing her to other members.

'You do ride I see from your, er, outfit?' said, Jack, a sprightly-looking old man in leathers.

'Well yes, of course, you think I dress this way all the time?' laughed Evelyn.

71

'What do you ride?' asked another.

'A Paggio Vespa 150,' replied Evelyn.

'Ah, 1977, single cylinder, two stroke,' he said in admiration, taking a peek out of the window. 'Nice little scooter.'

'Well, it's actually a later model,' Evelyn corrected him. 'Early 78.'

'What speed do you get out of her?' asked another.

'Oh, about eighty on the open road,' Evelyn replied, warming up to the interest and conversation.

'Good stuff!' said another. 'You must look after her.'

'Yes, I do,' she replied. 'I have a pet mechanic who's an absolute gem, loves vintage bikes, er, scooters.'

'Looks just like the one Audrey Hepburn and Greg Peck rode around Rome on in *Roman Holiday*,' one elderly lady said nostalgically. 'I loved that movie.'

'Well, the appearance hasn't changed much since then,' another man said. 'Classic design.'

'Of course I've had it modified; it's got disc brakes and an electronic ignition and it's an automatic CVT with torque server now,' Evelyn replied modestly.

'Wow,' the man said, obviously impressed. 'It looks like you've brought it up to a GTS300 model.'

The animated and enthusiastic conversation continued as Evelyn met and mingled. Eventually, she found herself ensconced with a cup of tea and a scone at one of the tables with a very jovial group of women. Idly she asked if there were any younger members or was it strictly over fifties and was told there was a younger chapter who only mixed occasionally on rallies and group outings. They had a different club room upstairs. Casually she asked if anyone knew a younger member by the name of Scott Warner. There was a puzzled response of denial until one man who'd overheard approached the table.

'Scott Warner? Wasn't he the young bloke who got into trouble with the law? Bashed his wife and was sent to prison?'

'Yes, I believe so,' said Evelyn.

'A friend of yours?' the man asked suspiciously.

'Oh, no,' Evelyn laughed. 'Hardly. I heard his name mentioned when I told a friend I was thinking of joining the club. He didn't seem my type at all so I was a bit dubious.'

'Nah,' said the man. 'I think he was a member of the upstairs chapter.'

'You can see our members are all very respectable,' said another lady at the table, rather primly.

'Oh, yes, definitely,' laughed Evelyn. 'I am relieved.'

'Well, have you decided if you're going to join?' asked Valerie.

'I'm certainly thinking about it,' replied Evelyn.

'They're all geriatrics,' Evelyn said to me the next time we were together. 'Nice folk, all very bright eyed and bushy tailed, but couldn't see any sign of sex, drugs and rock and roll.'

'Maybe you'll have to join up and snoop around the younger division,' I replied.

Evelyn had sent out the call sign immediately after she arrived home from her excursion. She was still wearing her bikie's moll outfit, which was a bit disconcerting.

'For God's sake take off that bloody wig,' I said. 'You look like a whore.'

She looked hurt at my reaction but grudgingly tore off the wig and threw it on the coffee table. 'Oh, I thought I looked very much the part,' she responded sulkily. 'You should've seen the reaction I got.'

I could well imagine.

'Anyway, I did join, I'll have you know,' she continued. 'We're off on a rally to Wangaratta next weekend. Apparently some of the younger division are coming with us; thought I might pick up a bit more information.'

'Oh, that's great,' I replied but I seriously suspected she was actually going because she wanted to.

'So, Warner's wife was found dead in the bath,' I continued. 'I dropped over there to have a look around but didn't come up with much except to learn that Warner was actually released about a month ago. Early release for good behaviour. But he hasn't been seen since, never arrived home apparently.'

'Neighbours didn't like him much either, I gathered,' Evelyn reported. 'Serial basher by the sound of it.'

'It's just the drowning in the bath that's suspicious. Very familiar MO and he now fits the time frame. The boys have got an APB out on him.'

'Well, if you don't mind, I'd like to have a shower and get rid of this makeup,' Evelyn said. 'These false eyelashes are driving me crazy.'

'Oh, and they look so sexy, Pixie,' I lied.

She gave me a look and disappeared towards the bathroom.

Tony was waiting for me when I arrived back.

'I've been looking through your active case files,' he said.

'And?'

'You didn't mention the Sheila Turner case.'

I'd forgotten all about that one. It had been going on for months. Sheila Turner had been a suspected suicide case but I had a gut feeling there was more to it than that. There were two possible suspects as far as I was concerned: her ex-boyfriend, Bruce, and his new girlfriend, Natasha. Apparently Sheila was distraught about losing Bruce and had a few too many drinks and climbed into the bath. It was claimed that her hair dryer, which was switched on, was lying on the shelf above the bath and it either fell or she knocked it into the bath and electrocuted herself. Well, it would've been quick. They found a pale line and blisters on the body at the water line so it was definitely electrocution.

The officers also found a couple of empty vodka bottles and several glasses in the drainer; no fingerprints except for Sheila's, which they found on a glass in the bathroom. I always thought it was an unlikely thing to do. Surely no one would have a live hairdryer so close to the bath. Still, she had been drinking. If it was suicide, why didn't she just take a handful of sleeping pills?

It suddenly hit me; she committed suicide in the bath! Bath deaths were not all that common but seemed to be becoming the latest fashion for dying. Her fingerprints were also all over the dryer and both Bruce and Natasha had alibis, albeit dependent on each other. They were supposed to have spent the night together at Natasha's apartment a couple of miles away. A neighbour had heard the unmistakeable erotic sounds of the couple coupling and complained to the manager. They both went up to the apartment and confronted the sexual gymnasts who apologised and promised to keep the noise to a minimum.

We'd questioned Bruce and Natasha several times and I'd let them know I was dubious about their stories and although Natasha seemed genuine, Bruce appeared very arrogant and shifty. I let him know in no uncertain terms he wasn't out of the woods and vowed I'd find out the truth. He was a big guy, too. He towered over me and told me I was wasting my time and to forget it if I knew what was good for me. Another suspect for the attack on me? I'd have another look at that. Boy, they were coming out of the woodwork, weren't they? I didn't realise so many people hated me.

I asked Tony about the twin brothers and it seemed they'd dropped right out of the picture but he would stay with it.

Thinking about the Sheila Turner case, I decided to have a word with Evelyn and see if she could do some snooping for me.

She'd just got out of the shower and was looking much more like her old self, thank God. She wrapped a pink, towelling bathrobe around her and was in the middle of drying her hair as I explained the story.

'God, give me a break,' she said. 'I can only work one case at a time.'

'But all I want you to do, when you're up to it, is see if you can have a word with the neighbour and check out his story. In his statement he said that he'd definitely seen Natasha and Bruce when he knocked on the door to complain about their noisy nuptials. He said they were giggling, shouting and squealing, and thumping the bed head on the walls something terrible. He actually complained to the manager saying they'd kept him awake all night and they both went up to the apartment to complain.'

'Oh, alright,' Evelyn sighed, resignedly. 'Give me his name and address. But I'll tell you now, it won't be today. I'm buggered after that trip to Broadmeadows.'

Chapter 8

Evelyn was lucky to find a parking spot in a side street just off Toorak Road, a few blocks away from the South Yarra address Lucky had given her. She was wearing what she described as her 'pathetic old lady' disguise, which consisted of a pink and lavender floral frock, longer than fashionable, a darker pink cardigan, and black flat-heeled court shoes. She teamed this with a grey knitted skull cap and simple single-pearl earrings. To cater for the Vespa, she had to hoist her skirt up around her waist while driving leaving a wide expanse of pantyhose on view. Not a pretty sight.

She dismounted, adjusted her skirt, retrieved her black handbag from the storage compartment and placed the keys inside. She pushed a couple of coins into the parking meter and set off.

As she approached the apartment block, a young couple emerged. They were laughing and holding hands. They didn't spare her a passing glance and continued on their way towards Toorak Road. Evelyn entered the apartment block before the security door swung closed and approached the reception counter, which was manned by a little mousey blonde.

'Can I help you?' the blonde asked, flashing a polite smile which exposed her dentally enhanced ultra-white teeth.

'Yes,' Evelyn returned the smile with her yellowing set of dentures. 'I'm looking for a Mr Stanley Boucher. What apartment number is he?'

'Number 6,' the blonde answered. 'Is he expecting you?'

'Oh, yes, we're old friends. Number 6? Isn't that next to Bruce and Natasha's apartment?'

'Yes, that's right. You know them too? You just missed them. You must've passed them on your way in.'

'No, I probably came from the other direction. What a pity.'

'You're not from the police, are you?' the girl asked suspiciously.

Evelyn smiled self-deprecatingly. 'Do I look like it? Why do you ask?'

'Well, apparently they've been interviewed a few times about Mr Curlew's ex-girlfriend who committed suicide a while back.' She leaned forward and whispered conspiratorially. 'Bit fishy, I'd say.'

'Oh? Why do you think that?'

'Very convenient, if you ask me. He's too good looking. He's just like all those other footballers, great body, sex crazed, orgies, drink, drugs, the lot.' She gave Evelyn a knowing look. 'Still, he did have an alibi, I suppose,' she admitted.

'A footballer?'

The blonde nodded disapprovingly. 'AFL – All Fun and Lust.'

Evelyn leaned in a little closer and lowered her voice. 'Well, to tell you the truth, I'm actually Sheila's mother and I agree with you. I want to check on that alibi with Mr Boucher. No one saw Mr Curlew leave the building that night?'

'No. Mr Bright, the manager – or manageress –' she giggled, 'was on duty that night. He was the one who took the complaint from Mr Boucher about the noise. They both went up together.'

'So the reception was left unattended?'

'Only for a couple of minutes and Mr Bright and Mr Boucher both saw them up in the apartment. You can check with Mr Boucher. I know he's in, I just saw him go up in the lift.'

'Oh, thank you, first floor, is it?'

'That's right,' said the blonde. 'Good luck.'

Evelyn nodded and made her way to the lift.

Stanley Boucher confirmed the alibi. He was a prim little man with a balding head and watery eyes.

'I'm sorry, Mrs Turner,' he said, 'but Mr Bright and I both confronted them. He was definitely there. Natasha opened the door.' He blushed. 'She was wearing one of those short see-through nightdresses.'

'And what was Mr Curlew wearing?'

'He was – naked.' He blushed again. 'I only saw his back and heard him talking. It was him alright, I've seen him enough.'

'Naked?' Evelyn couldn't resist.

'No, of course not!' Mr Boucher was affronted at the thought.

'But you didn't actually see his face?'

'Well, no, as I said, but I saw his back and I heard him asking what the problem was. I was standing behind Mr Bright's shoulder.' He paused again. 'He was wearing a pair of ladies knickers on his head, like a hat.'

'Who, Mr Bright?'

'No, Bruce Curlew,' he said, uncomfortably. 'It was all a bit disgusting. I had to turn away.'

'I can imagine,' Evelyn agreed, sympathetically. 'Did Mr Bright see Mr Curlew's face?'

'Well, I think he must have. As I said, he was standing in front of me and he was very flushed when we left.'

'Mr Bright is gay, isn't he?'

Mr Boucher blushed again and became very flustered.

'I really couldn't say. It's not really my business what people's sexual orientation is.'

'No, of course not. Sorry, I didn't mean to offend and you're quite right.'

'I mean, nobody cares these days, do they?'

'Only if you're a politician,' she laughed.

'Oh, no, he's a manager,' Mr. Boucher said, seriously.

'And when did you see Bruce Curlew next?'

'Not until the next morning when he and Natasha returned from breakfast. He stopped at the reception desk where I was collecting my mail and apologised for disturbing me the night before and promised it wouldn't happen again. Well, it had been the second time in a few weeks. I said I sincerely hoped it wouldn't and they went back up to their apartment.'

Evelyn thanked him for his co-operation, descended to the ground floor in the lift and headed to the front entrance. Passing the reception counter, she noted a hand-written notice announcing, 'Morning Tea. Back in ten minutes.'

Great security, Evelyn thought.

She inadvertently found herself in the wrong lane to make a right-hand turn into Toorak Road so, sensing she was being directed by her guide, she continued and turned left. A little way along she noticed a pavement café and sitting at one of the tables was the young couple she'd seen as she entered the apartment block. Recognising them as Bruce and Natasha, she pulled in to a parking spot that was just being vacated by a Mercedes Benz. She dismounted, slung her helmet over the handlebars, secured the lock and strolled back to the café.

She ordered a cappuccino from the waitress and sat at the table next to the young couple, straining her ears to pick up any conversation. The couple chattered small talk and the waitress brought the coffee. Evelyn took out her mobile phone and pretended to be making a call but she was actually taking a photograph of the couple as she pretended to chat on the phone. She finished her coffee and was about to leave when a tall, well-built, curly-headed blond young man approached Bruce and Natasha's table, greeted them heartily and sat down to join them.

Evelyn snapped another photograph of the handsome new arrival and settled back into her chair trying to overhear their conversation. It all seemed innocent enough with the men discussing an upcoming football match and their position on the AFL ladder. The blond young man took a folded sports magazine from his coat pocket and laid it on the table in front of Bruce.

'Check out the article on page seven,' he said.

Without looking at it, Bruce picked up the magazine and slid it into his own pocket. They chattered for a few more minutes and the young blond man got up, smiled at Bruce, kissed Natasha on the cheek and left.

'See you, Alec,' she said.

On the way back to her scooter Evelyn stopped at the roar of an oncoming motor cycle and was forced to step back to avoid being hit. The bike swung into the middle of the road to pass and she noticed it was being ridden by the young man with the blond curly hair sticking out from under his helmet.

'You've done extremely well, Evelyn,' I said as I studied the photographs Evelyn had downloaded from her computer. 'You're a natural investigator.'

Evelyn allowed herself a satisfied smile as she filled the electric kettle at the sink.

'So Stanley Boucher didn't actually see Bruce's face?' I said. 'That's not what he said in his statement. He said he definitely recognised him.'

'Apparently not. He claims he only saw him from the back and recognised his voice.'

'And Bruce was stark naked and Natasha was in a see-through nightdress? A bit distracting I would've thought, to both of them.'

'Well, the other witness, the manager, Mr Bright, is apparently gay so I doubt if he was looking at Bruce's face even if he did turn around.'

'But they both claimed it was only a brief confrontation and the reception desk was only left unattended for a couple of minutes, tops.'

Evelyn nodded.

'But if it wasn't Bruce,' she said, 'but somebody impersonating him, the real Bruce could've been hiding and slipped out and left the desk when Boucher rang him to complain.'

I pondered for a few moments, unconsciously levitating from the chair as I did so.

'I wish you wouldn't do that,' Evelyn complained. 'It makes me remember you're only a spirit and not as real as you usually appear.'

'Sorry,' I apologised and slowly descended back onto the kitchen chair. 'I'm still not used to this yet. I don't have the control I'd like. And this Alec character,' I said returning to the subject, 'you didn't get a surname?'

Evelyn shook her head.

'By the sound of it he was a footballer too. No idea what team? Probably the same as Bruce.'

'We really need to get a few answers, don't we? I mean there's no point my questioning anyone, they never see or hear me. We need to reopen the investigation. I don't suppose …'

But Evelyn cut me off.

'Don't expect me to go to the cops. They treat all psychics as interfering publicity hounds or deluded, weirdo idiots. Been there, done that.'

'But you wouldn't have to claim you were a psychic. You could tell them you'd just happened to be talking to this Boucher character and he mentioned he actually hadn't seen Bruce's face on the night in question. And you could tell them you'd seen Bruce, Natasha and this Alec guy having coffee together.'

'That wouldn't prove a thing and the cops hate anyone interfering, especially psychics, you know that.'

'But they might just interview Boucher and the manager again. What Boucher told you is different from his statement. It's possible that this Alec guy or somebody impersonating Bruce on the night gave Bruce an opportunity to slip out while the manager was away from the desk and do the dastardly deed.'

'I admit they're roughly the same build,' Evelyn mused, 'but Alec is blond and Bruce has black hair. Surely they would've noticed that through the knickers Bruce was supposed to be wearing on his head?'

'You said they were both naked or near naked. Now with two elderly old men, and one of them gay, surely that would've been distracting to a degree. As for the hair colour, ever hear of a rinse or a dye job?'

'But Alec's voice doesn't sound a bit like Bruce's.'

'A tape or CD? Didn't Boucher say this was the second complaint? Maybe the first time was a recording session.'

'But how would Bruce get back into the apartment block and Alec get out without being seen?'

I had to think about that one.

'Well, you said the security wasn't all that tight.'

'During the day,' Evelyn said, switching off the electric kettle which had started to whistle. 'What you're suggesting all sounds like a very involved conspiracy, wouldn't you say?'

'Murder nearly always involves a conspiracy,' I said, 'otherwise we wouldn't need investigators like me – or us,' I added.

'But why would he go to all that trouble just to dump a girlfriend?' she asked. 'He could've done it much easier by text or on Facebook. Everybody's doing it nowadays.'

'I don't know! I just had this feeling when I interviewed him. Something wasn't right. Maybe Sheila had something on him and was threatening to expose him,' I suggested.

'Now who's being psychic,' she said with a patronising smirk. 'You want a coffee?'

I gave her my famous wry look.

'No, I don't suppose it would work for you, would it?' she said as she took a single mug from the cupboard.

As she heaped four teaspoons of sugar into her coffee and sipped it appreciatively, a thought suddenly occurred to me.

'Did this Boucher character mention what Bruce was wearing when he saw him the next morning?'

She took a swig of coffee looking at me over the rim of the cup and swallowed.

'No, that wasn't on the list of questions you gave me. Why?'

'Oh, just wondered.'

'You want me to find out if he remembers?' she said in a weary voice.

'Oh, no, I was just asking,' I replied nonchalantly. 'Don't want to put you to anymore trouble for an investigation you don't seem to think worthwhile.'

She sighed heavily and went into the living room and returned with a phone directory which she began to flip through. She found the number and dialled.

'Oh, hello, Mr Boucher? This is Nancy Turner, we spoke this morning.'

She listened while he obviously recalled their conversation.

'There was something else I meant to ask you – do you happen to remember what Bruce Curlew was wearing the morning you saw him at the reception desk while you were collecting your mail the morning after the incident?'

She listened while he attempted to remember and then recalled the memory.

'I see, yes, it was cold at that time,' she agreed.

She glanced over at me across the mouthpiece of the phone.

'A pair of slacks, sports shirt and sweater ...' she repeated, and paused while he continued speaking, '... and a long leather overcoat over his arm.'

She listened for a few moments, muttering, 'I see' and 'uh huh' occasionally. 'Well, thank you, Mr Boucher, that's been a great help, thank you.'

She hung up the phone and smiled across at me.

'A long leather overcoat. Well, well.'

Chapter 9

Evelyn managed to get Sheila's mother's phone number and address after trying several Turners in the phone book. She knew she had the right one when she asked the woman who answered if she was related to Sheila Turner and the woman hung up. She hopped on the scooter and headed for Toorak.

The address was a very expensive home in an upmarket area. Evelyn was pretty certain the neighbourhood hadn't ever had the pleasure of seeing a 1977 Vespa in the area before, going by the inquisitive stares she got from the neighbours and passers-by. As she putted to a stop, she removed her helmet but didn't bother to secure it to the handlebars. It seemed unlikely anybody would bother stealing it or the scooter in this neighbourhood, unless they decided to have it towed away to the dump. Evelyn had dressed in her smartest brown slacksuit and tied a gold-striped silk scarf over her head to hide her black skullcap. She felt she was looking pretty spiffy.

She rang the front doorbell and heard the echo of what sounded like the chimes of Big Ben from within. The door was opened by a very smart, middle-aged lady also wearing a slacksuit, an orange designer-slacksuit, which put Evelyn's to shame.

'Mrs Turner?'

The woman nodded uncertainly spying the motor scooter parked on the kerb.

'Sheila's mother?'

Mrs Turner's face hardened.

'Are you the person who rang earlier? Are you a journalist?'

'Heavens no,' Evelyn laughed. 'My name's Betty Boucher, the sister of one of the witnesses in your daughter's case.'

'The one who gave that awful footballer an alibi?'

'Yes, that's right. We were talking about the case the other night and he let slip something that might be of interest to you.'

'I don't think so, Ms Boucher,' the woman said sullenly. 'My daughter committed suicide and that's the end of it. She chose her way of life against all the advice we gave her and she paid for it. Now, if you'd just leave me in peace …'

She went to close the door but Evelyn put her hand out and stopped her.

'But there is a chance that your daughter was murdered.'

Mrs Turner stopped and stared at Evelyn. Her expression changed to one of shocked uncertainty.

'You'd better come in,' she said, brusquely, and reluctantly stood back for Evelyn to enter.

They sat in the expensive and tastefully furnished living room but Mrs Turner didn't offer any refreshments. Evelyn described the conversation she'd had with Boucher and pointed out the difference to what he'd said in his statement.

'I think that's hypothetical,' said Mrs Turner. 'Surely they would have recognised that awful man. He isn't easy to forget.'

'You didn't approve of him or his relationship with your daughter?'

'Good heavens, no,' she replied 'He was arrogant, ignorant, with too much money, too much testosterone and absolutely no morality.'

'Apart from that, he was a footballer,' Evelyn couldn't help adding.

'Exactly,' Mrs Turner said with distaste. 'He ruined Sheila's life and as a result, we finished up having no contact at all.'

Suddenly Evelyn heard a voice in her head from the other side: 'You're wasting your time with her,' it said, 'she couldn't give a stuff about me and for God's sake don't tell her you're a psychic, she'll throw a fit and drag out her bloody rosary and crucifix.'

Evelyn also had a distinct feeling that Mrs Turner wouldn't be conducive to communicating with spirits or anything supernatural but she pressed on.

'But if there's even a chance your daughter was murdered, surely it would be worth your while to go to the police and ask them to reinvestigate? I'd be more than happy to go with you.'

Mrs Turner stared at her coldly for some time and then turned her head away.

'My husband is overseas on business at present but I'm sure I speak for us both when I say it was almost twelve months ago. Sheila is dead and buried – well, cremated. Nothing will bring her back.'

'But murder – surely you owe her a proper investigation.'

'And publicity, and court cases, neighbours and friends staring and whispering? I don't owe her father or me that again. It was horrible, you can't imagine.'

'Yes, I can,' Evelyn said, sympathetically, 'but …'

'No! I'll have none of that again. Now, if you'll please leave.'

She stood, indicating the conversation was over and ushered Evelyn to the door.

'Thank you so much for coming, Ms Boucher,' Mrs Turner said, graciously, 'but I think it would be better to let sleeping dogs lie.' She opened the door to let Evelyn pass and said, 'If, as you suggest, that awful man is guilty, then I am sure God will take the vengeance he deserves.'

Maybe so, thought Evelyn, as she walked down the steps and headed for her scooter, but I think He might be asking us for a bit of help. God does not always work alone.

Well, so much for a mother's love, she thought, as she climbed back on the seat and started the motor. 'Let sleeping dogs lie. It looks like we have to go this one alone,' she muttered to herself. 'Oops, with your help, of course, Big Boy,' she said, raising her eyes to Heaven.

On the way back home she had a sudden impulse to call into the police station. Maybe she could do something to convince them to re-open the case without revealing her source of information. She'd have to be very careful not to let them know about her connection with their dead comrade or the afterlife. A plausible story began to form in her mind.

She wandered into the station and directly to the counter where a young female constable was sitting.

'I'd like to speak with Superintendent Blake please, if that's possible.'

'Your name, madam?'

'Marsh, Evelyn Marsh.'

'He's very busy at the moment,' the constable said without checking. 'Can I help you?'

'No, I have some information relating to the Sheila Turner suicide which may interest him. Would you ask if he could spare me a few moments, please?'

'I'll see if he's available.'

The young constable disappeared into a back office. Evelyn studied the wanted posters and any other printed matter attached to the walls as she waited. The constable returned and ushered her into the office she had just left.

'Superintendent Blake will see you now. This way, please.'

Evelyn entered the office and the constable closed the door behind her as she left. Blake stood and indicated a chair opposite his desk. Evelyn sat just as the door opened again and another plain-clothes officer entered, nodded at Evelyn and walked around to stand next to Blake.

'Ms Marsh, this is Detective Sergeant Howell,' Blake said, indicating the officer beside him. "I believe you have some information relating to the Sheila Turner's suicide? The investigation is actually closed so how can I help you?'

'Stanley Boucher, Bruce Curlew's neighbour, and Mr Bright, the manager of the apartments,' she said. 'I believe they gave you incorrect information when you interviewed them regarding the whereabouts of Bruce Curlew, Sheila Turner's ex-boyfriend, on the night she died.'

The two officers shared a glance at each other.

'And why would you say that, Ms Marsh?'

'Well, I just happened to be talking to my friend, Mr Boucher, the other day about the case and, in passing, he mentioned the night in question. He informed me that he didn't actually see Mr Curlew's face when he and Mr Bright confronted them. He only saw the girlfriend, Natasha, and the man's naked back, and heard his voice.'

The two policemen shared another glance.

'And Mr Bright?'

'Apparently he was standing just in front of Stanley – Mr Boucher – and Stanley doubted if Mr Bright would have been looking at the man's face when he turned around. Er, it would appear Mr Bright is gay.'

She let the inference sink in while Blake just stared thoughtfully at her, and then continued.

'So he was probably more interested in looking ...'

'Yes, I get your point, Ms Marsh,' Blake interrupted, 'but as I recall both witnesses' statements confirmed Mr Curlew's identification.'

'They said they recognised him but didn't actually see his face. He was naked and wearing a pair of ladies' knickers on his head like a hat with his back to them and they heard his voice so they automatically thought it was Mr Curlew.'

There was a knock on the door and the constable entered carrying a couple of files which she laid on Blake's desk then

90

withdrew. Howell picked up the files and casually flipped through them, occasionally pausing to read something more closely. He then laid the open files in front of Blake indicating relevant passages and Blake browsed through them.

At that moment I arrived in the office slipping in before the constable closed the door. I could have gone straight through the wall but old habits die hard. Evelyn was so focused on the two detectives she wasn't aware of my presence, or if she was, wasn't prepared to show it. I settled down on the floor behind her and listened. Blake skimmed through the files glancing up at Evelyn from time to time.

'So you're suggesting that Mr Curlew could have slipped out, driven around to Ms Turner's place, got her drunk on vodka, filled the bath, stripped her off and threw her hairdryer in with her?'

'Something like that, yes.'

'You don't think it would have been easier to simply break up with her by telephone, email or texting her? That seems the most popular method these days. Murder seems a little extreme.'

'But maybe she had something on him and was threatening him.'

'For example?'

Evelyn wasn't quite sure but made a stab at it.

'I don't know – drugs, steroids, maybe a sex orgy he was involved in. That goes on a lot in football circles, I'm told.'

Blake smiled cynically. 'Have you had any personal experience with that sort of thing?'

'Don't be ridiculous,' she replied indignantly.

'And who was this mysterious friend you claim was impersonating him? Obviously somebody he knew very well. I mean, well enough to let this friend cavort around stark naked with his latest girlfriend while he was out murdering his former girlfriend.'

91

'Well, that's just the thing,' Evelyn replied, obviously getting into her stride. 'I just happened to stop for a cup of coffee in Toorak Road and saw Bruce and Natasha – Mr Curlew and the new girlfriend – at the next table.' She rummaged around in her handbag and took out the photographs she'd taken of the couple and handed them across the desk to Blake.

Blake's expression was cynical. 'And that made you suspicious? What kind of coffee were they drinking, vodka cappuccino? He doesn't seem to be naked,' he said sarcastically as he re-studied the photograph.

'No,' she scoffed, 'it was a very cold day. The point I'm making is they were joined by a friend,' she indicated the second photograph, 'a curly-headed blond man about the same size and build as Mr Curlew, probably one of his football mates.'

Blake pretended to be fascinated by her story.

'And this is the friend you suspect was impersonating Mr Curlew while he was playing hide the baton with his present girlfriend?' He looked at the photograph closely. 'Funny, but Mr Curlew has dark curly hair and his friend is very fair, wouldn't you say? And they don't look anything similar apart from their size.'

'He was wearing a pair of women's knickers over his head,' she reminded him. 'and he could've dyed his hair. If Mr Boucher was right, they only saw him for a few seconds and they were probably shocked at the state the couple were in and assumed it was Mr Curlew.'

I could see this wasn't going anywhere so I decided to give her a bit of assistance.

'Tell him about the overcoat and not being seen until the next morning.'

This obviously jolted Evelyn because she suddenly shot upright and twisted her head around looking up at the ceiling, knowing I was there but not able to see me.

'And he had a long leather overcoat,' she blurted out.

'A long leather overcoat,' Blake repeated slowly. 'I don't see it in the photograph. Hanging over another chair, was it?' he said sarcastically.

'No, I mean the next morning, after Sheila was killed! Mr Boucher, Stanley, saw them coming back from breakfast and he was carrying a long leather overcoat. Bruce – Mr Curlew I mean, not Mr Boucher.'

Blake shook his head trying to follow her reasoning.

'What I'm saying is he was seen leaving with Natasha wearing the coat and when they returned he was carrying it over his arm. It could've been the imposter wearing the overcoat when they were seen leaving the apartment and Mr Curlew carrying it when they returned.'

She was obviously getting flustered so I intervened again.

'Tell him about the magazine the blond man gave him,' I said.

'Oh, shut up, Lucky!' she yelled, as she jerked her head again trying to look for me.

There was a sudden silence in the room with the two detectives looking askance at Evelyn.

'Are you alright, Ms Marsh?' Howell said.

'What?' Evelyn suddenly realised how strange her reaction to me must have looked. 'Oh, sorry, I have a condition that makes me do that sort of thing uncontrollably sometimes … Tourette's Syndrome.'

'Ms Marsh, or may I call you Evelyn? You've been involved in trying to help the police before, haven't you?' He referred to the other file on his desk. 'A case that involved the search for a young boy that went missing. The parents called you in for your psychic advice, didn't they? And the police spent a lot of time and money looking where you indicated the body would be found. It wasn't found, Ms Marsh, in fact it's never been found.'

Evelyn, now being identified for what she was, became even more flustered.

'I told you the killer moved it! To a place near a bridge, lots of trees and water, a riverbank! The body's probably been washed away in the floods by now.'

'That description could fit hundreds of places in Victoria, Ms Marsh,' Blake replied, exasperated and obviously annoyed by this stupid phoney. 'Do you realise the pain you caused those parents? You've been using your psychic powers to sleuth again, haven't you?'

He raised his voice to a stern warning tone. 'Sheila Turner committed suicide. Case closed. If you continue to interfere with police business and investigations, I will arrest you for interfering in police matters and you will be thrown into prison. Is that clear?'

'But I just want you to check,' Evelyn protested, 'find out who this blond man is and search his home. He would probably keep the tape or CD they made of Bruce's voice, the one Mr Boucher and Mr Bright heard in the room. He'd be sure to keep it as insurance or maybe even for blackmail. Check Bruce Curlew's leather overcoat for evidence!'

'Go home, Ms Marsh,' he said, dismissing her. 'I won't warn you again.'

A humiliated Evelyn was escorted to the front door of the police station by Detective Sergeant Howell. He took her arm politely but firmly as he opened the door for her. His touch was all she needed. She turned to him at the top of the stairs leading to the street.

'I believe your young son – Bevan, isn't it? – is having a bit of trouble at school, Detective Sergeant. Bullying is such a common problem these days in schools, isn't it? What's the bully's name?' she pretended to search her memory. 'Sacha? Well, you're a policeman, you should be able to advise Bevan the best way to handle bullying. Teach him how to stand up for himself, show him some defensive tricks.'

Homicide Detective Sergeant Howell smiled patronisingly at her.

'You're wrong there, Evelyn, no one would dare bully my son. Yes, his name is Bevan, but that wouldn't be too hard to find out. I'd know if he was having trouble, he'd tell me if he couldn't handle it. Nice try, now off you go and remember what Superintendent Blake said. Keep your conspiracies to yourself.'

'Of course,' Evelyn said innocently, 'Bevan mightn't mention it to you because of the extracurricular activities you're having with Sacha's mother – Megan, isn't it? That's what's causing the problem. Sacha doesn't approve of your relationship with his mother so he takes it out on Bevan. Your son can hardly talk about it with you, can he?'

Howell's face dropped and she knew she'd hit the mark. Turning, she started down the steps.

'Wait a minute,' Howell stopped her as she reached the bottom. 'In there, you suddenly yelled out, "oh, shut up, Lucky".'

She turned to face him.

'I told you I was having one of my Tourette's attacks.'

'Were you? We had a Detective Sergeant Lambert we lost a while ago, accidentally drowned in her bath, the same as Sheila Turner. Her nickname was Lucky. You're not comparing the cases and suggesting both of them were murdered? You aren't trying to tell me you're, you know, communicating with them?'

'Now why would you think that, Detective,' Evelyn smiled, innocently. 'I mean, you don't believe in that sort of thing, do you?'

Having retrieved what she felt was a little of her self-respect, Evelyn made her way serenely across the footpath and mounted her scooter.

A puzzled and somewhat shocked Howell watched as she revved the motor and pulled out into the traffic.

'Put on your helmet!' he roared.

Evelyn saluted him with a backwards 'up you' finger and disappeared into the outside lane.

Chapter 10

'That's it!' Evelyn declared with finality. 'If you think I'm going to run the risk of being arrested and imprisoned, you've got another think coming. I should have known at the very beginning to stay out of this. I'd disconnected myself from the spirit world and I was doing alright. Then you came along – uninvited, I might add – and dragged me into all this.'

'But you went off on your own without telling me. If I'd known you were going to front Superintendent Blake, I could have given you some advice on what questions to ask and how to phrase them. I've had experience in dealing with superior officers.'

'And you've had no experience in dealing with psychics,' Evelyn replied, frostily. 'You don't suddenly turn up without warning when I'm in the middle of a delicate conversation with a police officer and interfere. You frightened the shit out of me.'

She was sitting in the living room with a second gin and tonic in her hand and a bowl of cheese sticks nearby for fortification. I was sort of sitting in the chair opposite.

'Sorry about that, Evelyn,' I apologised. 'I really am. But I can't do this on my own. I'm only new at this being dead stuff. I don't have the contacts I need yet. I don't know where else to turn.'

'What about your guide and your guardian angels? They'll help you if you ask.'

'There hasn't been sight or sound of them, apart from Joseph, and he told me I had to work this out myself. It's part of some sort of test.'

'Well, I suggest you do a bit more exploring and see what's available to you up there. I'm out of it. You might have to move to a different level. According to Robert Monroe, you'd be on the focus 27 level, that's where most souls go directly after they die.'

'Robert Monroe? Focus 27? Who is he and what the hell is Focus 27?' I asked, somewhat confused.

'No, Hell is a different level,' she said, dismissively. 'Robert Monroe is the founder of the Monroe Institute,' she explained, over-patiently. 'Their aim is to enhance worldwide cooperative efforts in furthering the exploration of consciousness, expanded awareness, and discovery of self; very informative stuff. He spiritually studied the different levels of consciousness after death and gave them numbers. You're obviously at Focus 27 level.'

What the hell was she on about? She sounded like she was reciting a lecture. 'Exploration of consciousness and expanded awareness' sounded like an LSD trip she was talking about.

'Whatever,' I said. 'But you won't help me?

'Nope.'

'Well, that's that then,' I said. 'I suppose I'll have to look for another medium.'

'Don't call me a medium! I'm a psychic! Mediums talk to the dead.

'But I'm dead!' I shouted in frustration.

'Yes, but I'm not talking to you.'

'Oh, get over it,' I said and the next second I was back sitting at my desk.

I must admit I was devastated with Evelyn's decision not to help me pursue the case. The problem was I really liked her as a person; she was intelligent, wacky, funny, and outrageous with a dry sense of humour that suited my style. But in all fairness, I couldn't really blame her. I'd asked her to step out of her comfort zone. She'd been humiliated by the police and, although I didn't actually force her to see Superintendent Blake, I certainly contributed to it. I'd whetted her appetite and she simply followed through the best way she could. And she did pick up some interesting information.

I decided to check Evelyn's credentials and, once again, I hit the Akashik Web. Up came a website which gave me information on her life. It appeared she was born in Geelong, Victoria, to very kind and understanding parents, Joel and Charlotte Marsh. At a very young age, almost as soon as she could speak, she was observed talking to, what her parents put down to, her invisible friends.

This was not considered unusual as most children appear to form relationships with invisible friends but she spent a lot of her so-called conversations simply listening with a sort of detached look on her face. She would nod and agree occasionally and then respond. Some of the time she would turn her head as though following her respondent around the room. As she grew older the 'conversations' became more frequent until eventually her mother asked her to whom she was talking. Evelyn would respond in a very matter-of-fact voice that it was Judith or Susan or some other name.

Her mother would ask her to describe these other children and Evelyn would reply, 'They're not all children, Mummy, some of them are old. Grandma came to talk last night.'

Grandma had passed away years before Evelyn was born and her mother asked her to describe the lady to her.

'She was very short and very old with long straight grey hair and blue eyes and she wore a beautiful gold ring with a lady's face carved on it.'

'You mean a cameo?' her mother asked her.

'What's a cameo, Mummy?'

Her mother explained and Evelyn confirmed it was indeed a cameo; repeating the word to herself to set it in her mind. Her mother was shocked at this revelation because the description fitted her mother to a T, right down to the cameo ring, her mother's favourite. Instead of being worried about her daughter's frame of mind, Charlotte, who was a very astute and sensitive type, related the conversation and the claims to her husband, Joel, who, surprisingly, nodded sagely. 'Aye, she's got the gift. It runs in my family.'

Wisely, instead of attempting to dissuade Evelyn from talking about her 'friends', her parents encouraged her and explained it was very normal for some children to see and hear spirit entities but it was best not to talk about them to her school friends or other people and to keep it a secret between themselves.

Thus Evelyn grew up in a loving and supportive environment and when she became a teenager with no sign of a decline in the number of 'visitors' she conversed with, her father and mother took her to a local spiritualist church where she underwent psychic training.

This was not to say that her childhood was entirely free of criticism as she sometimes forgot her parents' advice and automatically conversed with departed souls in the company of other earthly people, and gained a reputation of being a bit weird. This hurt and confused Evelyn as she thought everybody could see and hear these entities she conversed with.

As the years passed she learned to control her visions and to fit in with 'normal' people. She developed a quick wit and an unshakeable faith in her gift and used it to help the living and the departed. She became familiar with her spirit guide, Angela, and developed her talents even further. She learned how to predict some things which were not always reliable, as she saw these predictions as indications of what would happen if the client remained on the same path. If, through the free will available to everybody, they or somebody else involved in the prediction suddenly changed the direction in which they were heading, the prediction could be avoided, so she found that predictions were not always set in stone and warned her clients of this.

However, people of a certain inclination needed reassurance and she did what she could to help. She also learned how to assist lost, earthbound souls to find their way to the afterlife plane and this was a joy which gave her much satisfaction but attracted a reputation that was not altogether helpful.

Thus it was that she was contacted by a middle-aged couple whose eleven-year-old son, had disappeared mysteriously late one weekend whilst playing in a nearby park. They had contacted the police and reported James missing and lived in fear of his being found dead or injured. Although a massive search had been undertaken, no sign of the missing boy had been discovered until eventually, in desperation, the parents had contacted Evelyn through a friend who had raved about her talents. Feeling the suffering and plight of the parents, she had reluctantly agreed to assist if she could.

She went to the park and Angela showed her the boy playing and his mates departing to go home leaving James alone playing on the slide. Angela then showed her a man in a white van pulling up beside the park and the man getting out and playing and talking to James in a friendly manner. After a while the man, in his late twenties or thirties and dressed in khaki work overalls, accompanied the young boy to his van, helped him into the passenger seat and drove off. Evelyn had felt a sense of deep evil over the scene.

She then saw a bush track near a rubbish dump with a sign that said 'Dumping of any Rubbish Prohibited' and a heavy earthmoving work machine standing idle nearby. She then saw the man dragging the boy's body out of the van and, taking a

101

red-handled shovel from the back of the van, digging a grave and burying the boy's body. This upset her enormously.

She tried to tell the parents that she was sorry but she was unable to help them but she was sure the lad was in good care now, meaning he had passed over and was with family and friends. She was unable to contact James directly as was sometimes the case. Maybe he hadn't learned how to communicate yet.

However, distraught at the hideous crime, she took to roaming the countryside on her motor scooter and under Angela's direction, finally found the spot where James had been buried. She notified the police and they were very contemptuous of her information based on the fact that they had received many calls from so-called psychics giving the location of James' body, some saying he was alive and being kept hostage in country New South Wales and others saying he was living with relatives in the Northern Territory.

After many weeks of failure to obtain any reliable information and desperate for leads, the police finally decided to follow up any possibility of finding the boy and asked Evelyn to take them to the spot she had found. They had already investigated several other so-called psychics without success and were very reluctant to continue along those lines of inquiry. However, at the insistence of a young senior constable, who had never dismissed the possibility of psychic assistance, he finally convinced his superiors to at least search the location, as a white van had been seen in the area on the day in question.

Almost the moment they arrived at the spot, Angela's voice came through loud and clear to Evelyn.

'He's been moved! The man has moved the body to the side of a creek, near the Goulbourn River!'

Evelyn immediately became desolate as she stepped from the police car.

Police personnel were already at work digging, without success, around the spot Evelyn had indicated. She approached the officer in charge and with great reluctance and embarrassment informed him that the body had been moved.

He turned to her with a look of disgust. 'Thanks a lot, Ms Marsh,' he finally said angrily. 'Do you realise how much trouble and expense you have caused us?'

And without another word to her he yelled out to the crew, 'Okay, boys and girls, another false alarm from another bloody psychic. Pack up and let's get out of here. I knew this would be another waste of bloody time.'

As he was leaving he turned to her and said cruelly, 'I hope you're satisfied with your fifteen minutes in the spotlight, madam.'

She was forced to withstand the disgusted looks from the police personnel as they returned to their vehicles.

Evelyn tried to explain that the body had been moved to somewhere near a creek on the Goulbourn River but the officer was in no mood to even listen to her. Utterly dejected, she decided she would never again put herself in this position and to relinquish her talents forever.

Now I understood Evelyn's reluctance to help me and I couldn't really blame her.

While I was perusing the list of psychics again for a possible assistant, checking their ratings and trying to get an idea of their personalities, Joseph suddenly appeared beside me. This time he was dressed in the uniform of the Police Commissioner! I thought that was going too far; a simple constable, or even a detective sergeant or superintendent would have been sufficient but no, he appeared as the bloody Police Commissioner! I automatically jumped to attention before I recognised who it was. But the clear, deep blue eyes, the dark curly hair, the broad shoulders and chiselled jaw were a dead giveaway.

He laughed. 'At ease, Senior Detective Sergeant. This is just for effect. We've got an appointment. How's the case coming along?'

I told him about Evelyn and the help she'd been and that she'd now decided not to go ahead with the investigation.

'Not to worry,' he said, dismissing my concerns. 'Things will work out the way they should. It takes a while to organise the different levels of assistance you'll need. Sometimes we have to tweak the paths of synchronicity. In the meantime,' he continued, 'you and I have another engagement.'

Seemingly an instant later we were hovering above a church. I immediately recognised it. It was St Mary's Anglican Church in North Caulfield, just off Glen Eira Road; our local church. It was a lovely old bluestone, French Gothic edifice built in 1871, surrounded by lots of large trees and gardens and built back from the road. It was a shame they never constructed the tower and spire from the original design. They ran out of money, I suppose, or sent it to England to be blessed and never saw it again. I remembered it so well from my childhood when Mother insisted we attend every Sunday, rain or shine. I loved the many beautiful, stained-glass windows and cast-iron internal columns with their elaborate capitals and cedar furnishings, which captivated me in my youth and almost convinced me to become a nun, before I became disenchanted with the whole religion bit when I entered the force and saw the seedier side of life.

Now as we looked down I could see a crowd of people standing around chatting and then I noticed an honour guard of police personnel and a coffin topped with a huge bouquet of beautiful waterlilies and iris being ceremoniously carried down the aisle between the lines of guards.

Oh, God, I suddenly realised, I'm at my own funeral!

Oh, Mum, why a church funeral service? Why not a celebrant at a barbeque or a picnic in the outdoors? You know I hate funerals anyway.

Drifting closer I saw my mother, dressed in designer funeral black, complete with lace veil of course. She was surrounded by 'the girls', also dressed in designer black but thankfully un-veiled, and all looking very suitably distraught and pious. My father stood, or floated, behind my mother with his arm around her shoulders as she wept silently.

The rest of the mourners were dressed much more casually, I was pleased to see: bright colours and mostly hatless except for the members of the force who were all in uniform and looking smarter than I remembered except for formal parades. I wonder what they dressed me in for the funeral. I hope it wasn't that pale blue twenty-first birthday number that Mum insisted I wear. It was skin tight over the bust and hips and flared out at the hem. The poor old undertaker would have his work cut out getting a dead body into that. I suppose he'd have to slit it up the back. Thank God the coffin wasn't open for viewing!

All my office buddies were there, bless 'em, from all ranks, and many I'd known from other divisions. Superintendent Blake was there, of course, as was Homicide Detective Senior Sergeant Howell. They scrutinised the crowd, no doubt checking to see if a possible murderer had turned up and by some miracle be able to identify him but it didn't look as though this would happen. Not a tall, broad-shouldered, tough-looking bikie wearing a grey balaclava to be seen.

I recognised many friends and a few distant relations and felt grateful they'd bothered to turn up. Then I saw Paul, looking appropriately sad, but the effect was spoiled somewhat by the beautiful Asian woman on his arm. She was gorgeous, naturally, and wearing a stunning red silk cheongsam, which I thought a trifle tasteless under the circumstances of the occasion. How could he flaunt his latest adornment at his ex-wife's funeral? I thought he was wearing Calvin Klein but I couldn't be sure. He looked beautifully elegant as usual in a dark grey three-piece suit but no tie; just a pink business shirt open at the neck.

And then, I suddenly noticed a plump lady dressed in a purple and lavender floral print dress, a gold pashmina and a black, wide-brimmed straw hat, standing around the corner of the church taking a nip from a brandy flask. It was Evelyn! She'd come to my funeral, bless her! She obviously sensed I was there and raised her hip flask in a toast to the departed.

The procession moved into the church following the coffin and the mourners took their seats in hushed silence as the beautiful organ played softly in the background. The service was being conducted by the Victorian Police Chaplain, and the eulogy was read in deep, moving tones by the Assistant Police Commissioner, not the absent Police Commissioner, I noted a little archly, and the words, 'dedicated, exemplary role model' and 'loved her job' and 'respected and admired police officer, duty before her personal life' and other platitudes rang out. I retreated back up to the roof. I didn't need to hear the story of my life; I'd lived it.

It was only then I noticed a host of other departed souls had joined me and there was much cheering and laughter and jolly conversation. I recognised deceased aunts and uncles, grandmothers and grandfathers, fellow police officers who had been killed in the line of duty or died of medical conditions, and friends who had lost their lives. They had all come to congratulate me on my former life! What a jolly party it was, catching up with past souls who had touched my life. Even Tony joined the party. We were having a lot more fun than the sombre lot in church.

Evelyn arrived at the Rusty Pistons Motorcycle Clubhouse very early in the morning, looking forward to the Wangaratta rally. She was amazed to find at least thirty motorbikes and scooters already gathered in the parking lot. Their riders were in high spirits, standing around in groups, laughing, chatting and drinking coffee from plastic mugs. As she dismounted, several members watched her with interest as she made her way towards them. From their midst she suddenly heard Valerie's voice raised in astonishment as she stepped from the crowd.

'Pixie, is that you?'

'Hi, Valerie, yes, it certainly is. Glad I'm not too late.'

'I hardly recognised you,' said Valerie. 'Where's the long red hair and the pile of makeup?'

Evelyn had decided to dress more conventionally for this excursion and had discarded her bikie moll image. Dressed in her warm, grey woollen baggy slacks, fair isle sweater, a rather smart, red knitted cap with the peak at a jaunty angle, black leather boots, jacket and her normal subtle makeup, she was almost unrecognisable; more normal looking, perhaps, but more acceptable for an over-fifties motorcycle club. Once the other members had recovered from the startling transformation, they greeted her effusively and began discussing the upcoming trip.

'Everybody got their multi-vitamins?' Valerie called to the group. 'We'll need them for this trip. It's a long ride and we don't want anyone falling off or going to sleep on the road.'

The other members confirmed they had taken their vitamins but Evelyn had taken her supply before leaving home so she didn't reply.

They would ride in a procession two bikes wide, stopping at Seymour for their first toilet break and coffee, then onto Euroa for a toilet break and maybe another coffee, then on to Violet Town for coffee and another toilet break, then Benalla for a repeat performance but no coffee, before heading to Wangaratta where, after possibly a four- or five-hour ride that would normally take two, they would stay overnight at a motel Valerie had booked and return the next morning to Broadmeadows. There would be a social get-together in Wangaratta with the obligatory barbeque and for those who could still stand up, a bush dance, followed by an early night.

Valerie and her husband, Bob, would ride the lead and the others would follow. 'Try to keep up, please,' Valerie ordered. 'You all have your maps and the more technically advanced, a GPS, so please do not take unspecified exits on the way which will lead to a time-consuming search party and possibly a late arrival in Wangaratta thus throwing out the carefully planned timetable Bob and I have organised. Thank you, Rusty Pistons, and enjoy the ride.'

'Rusty' being the operative word, Evelyn thought to herself.

As final discussions and instructions were being given, Evelyn was distracted by the loud arrival of four more motorbikes, all Harley Davidsons, ridden by three much younger and rougher-looking riders and a slightly older one in his late forties, by the look of the craggy face and wrinkled, weather-beaten skin. They were welcomed a little less enthusiastically by the other members and stood to one side separate from the main group.

Jack sidled up to Evelyn and whispered, 'They're our bodyguards, from the other chapter – the Silent Chapter.'

'Silent Chapter?' Evelyn questioned.

'Well, they're mostly the younger, tougher side of the Pistons. They keep mostly to themselves even though they're regular members.'

'Why do we need bodyguards?'

'They reckon we're too old to look after ourselves on the road,' he answered, 'so they always send a few escorts to keep us company in case of trouble. You know, like the One

Percenters suddenly turning up and scaring the shit out of us. Nice of them really, taking care of us oldies.'

Before he could explain any further, another Harley roared into the yard and parked next to the new arrivals.

'Well, they're being extra careful today,' Jack remarked. 'We usually only have a couple of escorts.'

The latest arrival dismounted and removed his helmet. Evelyn couldn't believe her eyes – she recognised the build and that thatch of blond curly hair. It was Alec, Bruce Curlew and Natasha's friend from the coffee shop! Well well well, she thought; a coincidence or a connection?

'Who's the young blond hunk, Jack?' she asked.

'That's Alec, one of the top blokes in the Silent Chapter. Wonder why he's on the ride today? Must be checking out the Wangaratta Wanderers; they're sort of a rival chapter. Pays to keep an eye on the competition.'

'Competition?'

Jack gave her a conspiratorial look, tapping his nose with his finger, but didn't elaborate.

'The others are Pete, the one with the shaved head, and Ruffo, the redhead with bushy beard, Digger, the ex Nam vet with the grey curly hair, and Jason, the older one, who's also a Nam vet. There's talk of Jason joining us now he's almost sixty,' he whispered conspiratorially. 'He's slowing down and doesn't seem as close to the others, sort of more withdrawn. He'd be better off with us oldies, I reckon. We'd soon cheer him up.'

The call to mount up was given by Bob and the group dispersed to their bikes and scooters. There were some pretty nifty outfits, Evelyn noted, with a slight touch of envy. Her old Vespa might have a bit of trouble keeping up but she'd give it a damn good try. Some of the wives were riding pillion and there was a lot of chiacking between some of the obviously old friends. Anyway, this was supposed to be a fun ride enjoying the

109

company of her peer group out in the country so it wouldn't be competitive.

With a roar of engines the group took to the road heading for the Hume Highway. From close to the rear of the procession, mainly due to her slightly slower speed, Evelyn noticed the couples sorting out their usual positions but the Harley riders spread themselves out through the line, each riding in the kerbside position.

There was only about one hundred kilometres to Seymour, their first stop. Evelyn soon settled in and really began to enjoy the ride, almost mesmerised by the wind buffeting against her body and helmet and the long ribbon of grey bitumen stretching before her as they escaped the suburbs and headed through the beautiful countryside. Once or twice a police patrol car passed them, slowed down and seemed to be scrutinising the riders as they passed. Seeing only a group of elderly bikers obviously out on a social outing, they passed with a wave.

As they approached Seymour after about an hour, she was ready for a break. A couple of minutes later the procession slowed down and came to a stop outside a rather nice roadside cafe with red and white gingham check plastic tablecloths and red chairs on the sidewalk and a large parking lot next door where they dismounted and parked. There were a few giggles as some of the lady riders raced for the toilet block followed by most of the men. Evelyn was in no hurry to relieve herself and made her way to the cafe where she ordered a cappuccino and a Danish and took it outside to one of the tables. She noticed four of the Harley riders sitting together at one table. The one Jack had said was called Jason was sitting alone at another table. Obviously he didn't feel comfortable sitting with the other riders so Evelyn decided to join him and get acquainted.

'Hi,' she said brightly, 'I'm Pixie, I don't think we've met?'

110

'Jason,' he mumbled, reluctantly introducing himself. 'Wouldn't you be more comfortable sitting with your own group?'

'Oh, I dunno, I like to mix with the Harley riders. I'm a huge fan of Harleys,' she smiled.

'What are you riding?' he asked.

'Oh, only a little Paggio Vespa 150 scooter,' she replied self-deprecatingly. 'Only a toy compared with yours.'

Luckily he rose to the bait.

'Get away! What year?'

'Nineteen seventy-seven,' she answered, as if a little ashamed.

Jason brightened considerably.

'My first motor,' he said appreciatively. 'Got it when I was sixteen. Loved that little scooter. Lost me virginity the first night I rode it. Yeah,' he said dreamily, 'that was some ride.'

'The scooter or your partner?' Evelyn laughed.

'Both,' he said, joining in her laughter. 'I picked her up at the pub and took her for a spin. I think it was the feel of the engine between her legs.'

'That'll do it every time,' she grinned. 'Maybe you'd like to come for a ride on mine sometime, bring back old memories.'

He looked at her sharply, trying to gauge if she was propositioning him, but Evelyn had innocently returned to her Danish and coffee.

'Want to run up to the Vietnam vets' monument while we're here?' he asked. 'I usually drop in and pay me respects.'

'Would we have time?' she asked. 'I mean, I thought it was just a coffee and comfort stop.'

'Plenty of time,' he said. 'It's just up the road a piece. And this lot will be here for another good hour or so by the time they all go to the toilet. We won't do the Memorial Walk, that'd take too long.'

111

Evelyn saw this as a chance to get to know Jason better and maybe pick up some information about the other Harley riders.

'I'd love to,' she said, finishing her coffee. 'You can ride pillion on the Vespa if you like. I'd better tell Valerie and Bob we're going. They might miss us or leave without us.'

'Fair enough,' he said, as he also stood to make his way to the other Harley riders.

Evelyn told Valerie and Bob where she was going and they seemed fine with it but reminded her they'd be leaving soon. On the way back to Jason she noticed he was having a bit of a row with the other four and although there were no raised voices, the intensity of the argument was obvious. Jason told them to forget it and that he'd had enough and would catch up with them later maybe.

Alec watched them speculatively as they wandered over to the car park and mounted the Vespa. There were quite a few catcalls as they drove off and Evelyn smiled and waved. The rider called Digger yelled out, 'Watch 'im love, he'll hang on to ya boobs for support!'

To which Jason replied with a middle finger salute.

The monument was a simple, curved stone wall with plaques representing the various divisions that had been involved in the war and was the entrance to the Memorial Walk. They dismounted and walked the length of the Memorial while Jason explained the history involved. He appeared much quieter away from the other Harley riders and became very circumspect,

'Lost a few good mates there,' he mumbled, 'and what for? We're back trading with them and now the Aussie tourists overrun the place. But they don't have to put up with the spikes in the pits and the bloody tunnels that honeycombed the country.'

'Did you ever go back?' Evelyn asked.

He stopped walking and turned to her.

'Are you bloody serious? There's no way I'd want to go back to that hellhole country. I was there for two years and hated every second of it,' he said bitterly.

'What about your other mates?' she asked.

'Bloody Alec's been over a few times but the mongrel was too young to ever fight there. Besides, he wouldn't want to spoil his pretty looks. It's pretty obvious why he goes …' he paused. 'Business.'

He went very quiet for a moment and stood with his eyes closed, obviously paying his respects to his fallen comrades. She watched him and realised there was a lot more sensitivity to this man than she expected.

Suddenly he opened his eyes and brightened up.

'We'd better be gettin' back,' he said and they made their way back to the scooter. 'Hey, you're a pretty good rider; you handle the scooter pretty well for a sheila.'

'Why thank you, sir,' she said with a smile.

'Might take you for a burn on the Harley when we get to Wangaratta, what d'ya reckon?'

'Sounds good to me,' she replied.

They rode back into town just as the rest of the group were getting ready to leave.

'That was a quickie,' yelled Digger, 'but at your age she can't expect much more, can she?'

Evelyn stayed on her scooter as the others mounted up and led the way as they pulled out onto the highway. She noticed the Harley riders, except for Jason, pulled into the exit lane that led to Shepparton. Obviously they weren't continuing on to Wangaratta. Making a sudden decision, she followed them at a distance as they sped up.

About fifteen minutes later she rounded a bend and they'd suddenly seemed to have disappeared. She kept going, hoping to catch sight of them at the next rise but there was no sign of them.

Then from behind she heard the roar of their engines as they sped up to overtake her. Jason's bike cut in front of her and she was forced to brake hard to avoid running into him. He dismounted and strolled back to her as the other three bikes came to a halt.

'I think you're going the wrong way, Pixie. Wangaratta's that way,' he said pointing.

'Oh, I thought it was this way,' she responded. 'I was just following you.'

'We're taking a little diversion,' he said. 'You'd better turn around and go back. The others will be missing you.'

'Oh, alright, sorry,' she apologised. 'I'm new at this rally stuff.'

He held his ground until she did a U-turn and proceeded back the way she'd come. Only then did the four riders continue on their way in the opposite direction. A little further on, Evelyn pulled to the side of the road and looked back. There was no sign of the four bikers. She dismounted, walked to the side of the road and sat under a large eucalyptus tree. There was definitely more going on here than met the eye. She closed her eyes, slowed her breathing and inside her head, she called.

'Evelyn here! You'd better get down here – now!'

Chapter 11

I was sitting at my desk in the office having just returned from a quick trip to Paris. I'd sat on the top of the Eiffel Tower without having to pay for it and sped through the beautiful boulevards. It was a shame I couldn't drop in to a café for a pastry and coffee but I didn't really see the point.

This afterlife lark has its advantages. I discovered all I had to do was picture myself in a place and in an instant, I was there! I'd also discovered I could switch time zones as well. I intended visiting other times in history when I got around to it; for instance, London in its heyday and maybe Rome, Jerusalem and maybe early New York.

Thought I'd skip the First Fleet out to Australia in 1788; it was a monstrous trip by all the accounts I'd read and I didn't really want to experience the suffering of the miserable seven hundred-odd convicts who were transported on the six vessels through mostly dreadful weather with a lack of privacy, fresh water, edible food and the torment of illnesses and disease and death. I'd always had an interest in history and often wondered what it was really like when it wasn't glamorised in written accounts by people who hadn't actually lived in the period or those who had romanticised it. You can't smell the odours or feel the weather or feel the actual hardship that was often the plight of our forefathers. Now I had my chance but I'd be very choosy.

My daydreaming was suddenly interrupted very loudly by Evelyn's call. She gave me her location and off I went. I found her sitting in meditation under a eucalyptus tree by the side of the road just past Nagambie. The same blue beam of light I had seen when I had first called on her led me directly to her.

'Hi, you called?' I said as I landed in front of her. 'I thought we weren't talking.'

'Something's come up,' she said.

She explained about the geriatric road trip and the Harley bikers and how they rode hidden in amongst the elderly group of riders to avoid being noticed by the police patrols and how they'd left the group at Seymour and taken off in the direction of Shepparton. She then told me how they'd stopped her from following them and forced her to go back and join the other group.

'And that's not all,' she continued, 'the leader of the Harley riders was none other than Alec, the guy I saw with Bruce Curlew and Natasha at the café in South Yarra! He's one of the head honchos of the Silent Chapter of the Rusty Pistons. Tough lot, keep themselves separate from the older members. Coincidence? I reckon they're delivering or collecting supplies of drugs and using the oldies and the bike rally as a cover. Maybe Alec's supplying to Bruce Curlew and Sheila found out and had to be silenced. What d'you think?'

'Possible,' I replied. 'Good theory. How far ahead do you think they are?'

'Can't be too far although they were speeding,' she replied. 'I'm sure you could catch up with them. You could maybe find out if I'm right and maybe get the location of the pick-up or drop-off. There's definitely something funny going on.'

'Right,' I said, 'see you.' I took off in hot pursuit.

Evelyn caught up with the others at Euroa where they'd pulled in for another pit stop. Valerie and Bob chastised her for leaving the group and she replied that she'd just taken a short excursion to have a look at a couple of tourist spots she'd wanted to see. She apologised and explained she couldn't stop to argue because she desperately needed a pee. She waved to Jason on her way to the public convenience and was glad she'd missed the queue as the others had already been to relieve themselves. Ah, the relief.

I saw the bikers almost immediately. They had pulled in to a winery just outside Shepparton. It was an early Federation-style building and the grapevines in the adjacent vineyard were loaded with young fruit. I hovered nearby to watch the riders, who dismounted and removed their helmets. The young blond that Evelyn had described, Alec, removed one of his saddlebags, walked up the front stairs and rang the doorbell. A middle-aged, almost bald, Italian-looking man opened the door and without a word being exchanged, Alec entered. His other three mates stationed themselves at the foot of the stairs, lounging against the wrought iron railing. So it looks like they were expected.

I quickly explored the grounds, noting the layout, then slipped through the front door, literally, and arrived in a sort of informal sitting room. Alec and the Italian guy had settled into armchairs. The saddlebag remained at Alec's feet. They exchanged pleasantries and the Italian finally got down to business.

'Alright, how much you got?'

'Only a kilo and a half, Nunzio, but there's more on the way.'

'When?' the Italian asked. 'I got orders to fill from here to the border.'

'Soon,' Alec replied. 'The end of the month. Another shipment is on the way.'

Nunzio grunted, obviously not happy with the news, and held out his hand.

'Show me.'

Alec bent, opened the saddlebag, removed a package and passed it to Nunzio.

The Italian stood and took it to a desk against one of the walls, removed a set of scales from one of the drawers and weighed the package.

'Good quality like usual?' Nunzio asked.

'The best,' Alec replied with a grin. 'Never a complaint.'

'Is just under one and a half kilos. You trying to rob me?'

Alec held up his hands in denial.

'Nunzio,' he smiled defensively, 'hey, you've been doing business with us for years. Would I do that to an old friend? You pay for what it weighs, as always.'

'Same price as last time?'

Alec nodded.

Nunzio grunted again, picked up a pencil from the desk and calculated the cost. He then slid open a panel beside the desk and revealed a safe. Checking over his shoulder that Alec wasn't watching him, he squatted and entered the combination, opened the safe door and withdrew a thick envelope of cash. He quickly counted out the amount, stuffed the remainder back in the envelope and returned it to the safe, closing the door and spinning the combination dial. He handed the cash to Alec who stood and thanked him.

'You put it down in the cellar like usual,' Nunzio said. Alec picked up the parcel and nodded. 'Roselia, she be home soon so be quick.'

Alec turned to go and at that moment he was confronted by a young man standing in the doorway.

'Hi, Scotty,' Alec said, slapping the other man on the shoulder in a brotherly greeting. 'How you doing, mate? Keeping your nose clean and staying out of sight?'

'I've got an option?' the young man replied.

My God, I thought, and I was glad they couldn't hear my intake of breath. But then again, I remembered I wasn't actually breathing, was I?

It's Scott Warner, my old adversary! The husband the cops are looking for about his wife who was drowned in the bath! How the hell did he get here?

'Any news?' Scott asked.

'Nah, the cops are still looking for you, mate. Just stay put for a while longer and we'll try and sort it out. Maybe a bit of plastic surgery on that ugly mug and a quick trip up to north Queensland, eh?'

'But I didn't do it!' Scott pleaded. 'I arrived home that night and there she was, in the bath, drowned! I knew the cops would think I'd done it because of my previous so I got out quick. I didn't know where to go!'

'Yes you did, Scotty,' Alec smiled. 'You came to us. And we took care of you, right? What are old mates for? Now just lie low for a couple more weeks till the heat's cooled down and we'll make our move, okay?' He ruffled Scott's hair in a playful, reassuring way and slapped him on the back again.

'It wasn't suicide, Alec, I know! Somebody drowned her! A man had been there, I could smell him.'

'Well, I'll tell the cops to look for a smelly guy with wet hands, eh?' he laughed.

'She'd been playing around while I was inside, I know. She was a beautiful woman. She'd never wait that long for me.'

'Well, if she was playing around, she got what she deserved, right?'

Scott's shoulders slumped, headed for the couch and collapsed onto it. Alec watched him.

'Keep yourself calm, Scotty. Get Nunzio to give you a sniff or two – charge it to us, Nunzio,' he said, turning to the Italian.

'I charge, don't you worry about that, 'Nunzio replied testily. 'Is bad enough him moping around the place under Roselia's feet all the time. I had to tell her he was the son of a relative from Italy. I don't think she believes me. She one smart signora.'

119

'But the pay's good, eh?' Alec smirked.

'I don't use the stuff, you know that,' Scott said dismissing the offer.

Nunzio grunted again and turned away. 'You go now.'

With another look at Scott, Alec turned towards the front door, stopped, turned back, collected the parcel and saddlebag and with a grin and a cheerful wave he left.

The trip to Wangaratta was uneventful apart from the scenery. Jason had taken to riding alongside Evelyn as her partner. He allowed her to have the inside position, which suited her fine. They drove into town in a cacophony of noise, startling the locals, who scattered out of the way as if they were being attacked by a mob of kangaroos instead of a herd of retirees. The group pulled up at the motel and Valerie allocated the rooms and who would be sharing. Evelyn drew Desley, a thin little sixty-three year old with grey hair and glasses which needed up-grading by a good optometrist. Evelyn was horrified and amazed that Desley had driven all the way without running into a tree or semi-trailer and thanked God she wasn't her ride buddy. It was going to be bad enough sharing motel room with her.

After she'd settled in, Jason offered Evelyn a ride on his Harley to show her some of the local sights. She accepted gladly and they roared off, first to Mad Dog Morgan's gravesite in the local cemetery where Jason, who was obviously a fan of the nineteenth-century bushranger and murderer, enthusiastically informed her that there was a lot of controversy about Morgan's real name. Some said it was Moran and others claimed it was Owen. He was definitely the illegitimate son of a Mary Owen and his father's name was Fuller. He got the name of Mad Dog because of, well, he was as 'mad as a cut snake' in Jason's words: bushranging, holding up cattle stations and holding the owners and workers as prisoners, killing cops; all good clean fun. He also told her there was an obscure relationship between Morgan and Banjo Paterson's 'Waltzing Matilda', Australia's unofficial National Anthem.

Apparently Mad Dog had held up the Peechelba Station and held everybody prisoner while he got drunk on the boss's rum. The station owner's wife begged him to let the nurse, one Alice Keenan, attend to the cries of her one-year-old daughter, Christina MacPherson, which he reluctantly allowed. Well, years later, the grown-up Christina moved to Winton in Queensland where she met Banjo Paterson and, according to legend, she hummed the tune of 'Waltzing Matilda' while he composed the lyrics. So if Mad Dog had shot the kid to shut her up, we may never have had the rousing tune that marks our nation at parades, celebrations and sporting events.

Jason seemed to know the whole story of Mad Dog and related it all in great detail up to the point where the bushranger was shot in the back when he was surrounded by the police and a posse of station hands. It was claimed he was shot by an employee named John Windlaw, but some said it was really a bloke called Quinlan.

During the telling of this story, Evelyn was enthralled with Jason's passion and found herself becoming quite intrigued by this strange, middle-aged, ordinary-looking bikie who obviously had the heart of a wild bushranger beating in his breast.

As a contrast he took her to the local art gallery and drew her attention to the aluminium cast artwork of a man's left hand which included a penis and testicles protruding from where the middle finger should be. It was beautifully crafted but Evelyn had to question the artist's impressionist motives. It also gave an entirely different interpretation to 'keeping your hand in' or 'pull my finger' or 'get your finger out' and thought it could be very handy to carry on her scooter for hand signals. Jason was obviously enthralled with it and the many other excellent works

121

of art on display. What a strange mixture of murder, mayhem and art this man was.

They visited the nearby Warby-Ovens National Park about ten kilometres from the town. At Ryan's Lookout they admired the beautiful landscape of old-growth red gums and box-ironbarks and the lower reaches of the Ovens River and they felt quite comfortable and at peace in each other's company.

The evening barbeque went well and one of the ex-rockers had brought an MP3 player with a collection of sixties and seventies hit rock tunes on it for those inclined to jive or rock 'n roll, the Twist being out of the question with the hip-replacement brigade. She and Jason sat together chatting on canvas deck chairs sharing the steak, sausages, salad and the obligatory pavlova, smothered in whipped cream and passionfruit, washed down by cold beer.

'Will you be going to the dinner dance at the clubhouse?' she asked Jason.

'When is it?'

'The twenty-seventh.'

He was immediately evasive. 'Oh, I don't think so, I have a sort of job on that night.'

'A sort of job?'

'Yeah, well, we've been told to make ourselves available for that night – well, ordered, really.'

Evelyn suddenly had an intuitive flash. She saw the water, a jetty, and a boat. It was night time, and the mental flash had a dark feel about it. It was bad enough for her to suddenly say 'Don't do it, Jason. I don't know what you're supposed to be doing but don't. It won't turn out well.'

He looked at her in surprise.

'What are you talking about? You don't know what the job is, you couldn't.'

'No, I don't know what the job is,' she replied, suddenly feeling stupid for bursting out with the warning but it couldn't be helped. She felt so strongly about it, 'I just know it's got a bad ending,' she added lamely.

He looked at her strangely and then laughed. 'Are you psychic or something?'

She shrugged, uncomfortably. 'I just have a bad feeling about it, that's all.'

'Don't worry, it won't be the first time I've done it,' he reassured her. 'But I can promise you it'll be the last. I've had enough. I'm getting out.'

'Then don't do it, quit now.'

He looked at her for a long time trying to figure out her reaction and then shrugged it off.

'You don't refuse an order or just pull out of my Rusty Pistons chapter without getting seriously hurt or dead.'

Any further conversation was halted by the roar of Alec's motorbike arriving on the scene.

Jason suddenly jumped up and invited her to attempt a shuffle on the grass dance floor but they were forced to retire after Jack cut in and tried to dance with Jason. She was not so happy she'd joined the Rusty Pistons Motor Cycle Club now. There was doom on the horizon.

Sharing the motel room with Desley was a bit of a strain and prevented Evelyn from inviting Jason back for a nightcap or any other diversion she might have in mind. She went into the small bathroom to prepare for bed when she noticed, among the lotions, creams, makeup and soaking dental plate that Desley had left scattered over the wash basin shelf, a small bottle of purple pills she thought she recognised.

'What are these, Des?'

'What?' Desley replied from the bedroom.

123

'The purple heart-shaped pills,' Evelyn answered.

'Oh, they're just my multi-vitamins. They're wonderful,' Desley called. 'You should get Valerie to get you some. We're all onto them. Make such a difference.'

I bet they do, Evelyn thought, as she replaced the amphetamines. So the lovely Valerie was supplying amphetamines to the oldies? Stranger and stranger.

'It's a bloody drugfest!' exclaimed Evelyn as we sat in the seclusion of the garden of the motel. 'No wonder they're all so jolly and energetic.'

'Well,' I said, 'I always reckoned it was the oldies that needed the drugs, anyway. So you think Valerie's supplying them?'

'Sounds like it.'

'I wonder where she's getting her supplies from? Probably Alec. Well he's definitely supplying to the Italian guy. I watched him take the package down into the winery cellar and hide it in a secret cupboard behind a sliding wine shelf. I get the feeling, though, that Alec's not the absolute head honcho. I think he's just the courier. The question is now, what do we do about it? And what do we do about Scott Warner?'

'An anonymous phone call to the cops?' Evelyn suggested.

'But that doesn't lead us to the killer. Scott Warner didn't murder me; he doesn't have tattoos on his arm. I definitely saw tattoos on the killer's arm. And I have a feeling he didn't kill his wife. I heard him back at the winery. He strongly denied it and there didn't seem to be any reason to lie to the blokes that were hiding him. I think we should nose around a bit more to see if we can pick up more information.'

'And then we can bust the whole operation.'

'When and if we find there's a connection with the killer.'

'I still think Alec's mixed up in the Sheila Turner killing,' Evelyn said with conviction. 'And he's obviously mixed up with the drug scene. I still think Sheila found out the extent of Bruce's involvement and threatened to expose him and that's why he killed her. And if Scott didn't kill his wife, who did and why? It's like a giant jigsaw puzzle. What's the full story?'

'Well, let's find out, shall we? I mean, if we're still talking.'

'You don't honestly think you can handle this on your own, do you?' Evelyn replied with a sniff.

'Who're you talking to?' Jason suddenly appeared beside her.

Startled, Evelyn turned. 'No one,' she answered. 'I was just thinking out loud.'

Jason walked up and sat on my lap so I moved away. 'See you later, Pixie.'

'We're all packed up to leave for the return trip,' Jason said to Evelyn. 'You ready?'

Chapter 12

That night I thought I'd investigate the upstairs quarters of the Rusty Pistons' Silent Chapter clubrooms to see if there was anything of interest lying around. It was as I visualised: untidy and dirty, with posters of naked women on and off motorbikes slapped on the walls, newspapers and magazines strewn about, overflowing ashtrays, discarded pizza boxes and takeaway food containers, and a couple of plastic bins overflowing with beer cans and bottles. In another room, apparently the office, stood an old desk with a laptop which was almost buried under papers and documents. A metal filing cabinet, vinyl office chair and a couple of old wooden kitchen chairs completed the furnishings. I started to look around, not really expecting to find anything of interest just lying around and suddenly I heard voices coming from the other room. Then the office light was switched on.

Alec entered first and it was apparent he was extremely angry.

'It's all right for you,' he snarled. 'I'm the one does all your dirty work and you sit back in your smart executive office and give orders and take the biggest whack of the profits!'

Then, to my total surprise, Paul entered, followed by the Asian girl he was with at my funeral! Paul, the respectable, well-heeled lawyer? My ex-husband! I couldn't believe it.

'Every organisation has its executives and its blue-collar workers, Alec,' he said calmly. 'The executives make the original investment, organise the supplies and take the risks. I'm the executive and you're the blue-collar worker. That's how it goes.'

126

The Asian girl walked serenely past the two men, seated herself on one of the visitor's chairs and crossed her shapely legs. She was wearing another silk cheongsam, a pale green floral number with the obligatory thigh-high split. It was amazing and a testament to their mood that neither of the men bothered looking at the wide expanse of shapely leg she displayed.

'Risks?' Alec shouted. 'You take all the risks? And what about me picking up the stuff and storing it and distributing it and being your own personal hit man and cleaning up your shit? I'm not taking risks?' he raged in utter disbelief.

Hit man? He said *hit man*! What the hell is he talking about?

'We came to an arrangement, a contract if you will, and you agreed to the terms,' Paul said, in that reasonable voice that brooked no argument, the voice that used to drive me crazy.

'Yeah, well, I didn't know it was going to involve me in murder!' Alec shouted as he ripped off his leather jacket and threw it onto the desk chair. He was wearing jeans and a white T-shirt which clearly displayed his broad shoulders, thick neck, bulging pectoral and arm muscles; arm muscles that were indelibly tattooed with blue and green snakes wrapped around a dagger and swirls of lines and Maori symbols! Alec was the man who attacked me in the bath! He killed me on Paul's orders? Why?

'Why did you want your wife killed, anyway?' Alec asked as if repeating my question. 'She was a copper! Coppers look after their own. It was a hell of a risk for me.'

'Yes, and you did a great job,' Paul said. 'Not a speck of evidence. I admit, you're a pro. Pity you left those red marks around her neck and shoulders, though, otherwise it would've been put down to accidental drowning. It nearly always is. But there's nothing to tie you in to her killing.'

'The bitch struggled! I had no option. I was lucky she didn't scratch me and leave my DNA under her fingernails. Luckily I had plastic gloves on and the water made my hands slippery.'

'As I said,' Paul smiled, 'you're a real pro. You know I couldn't take the risk. She'd told me she was working on a drug case and from what I'd heard, it sounded like it was ours. She had some bloody informant she'd met up with but although you got to him first, I was watching and he was still alive when she found him. That was a big mistake, Alec, you should've made sure you'd finished the job before you drove off. That wasn't so professional.'

Alec almost looked embarrassed but didn't defend himself. Paul continued.

'She never told me what his dying words were but I suspected he'd said enough to throw suspicion on me and our operation. By that time we were beginning to split up and we weren't talking much. She was very reticent about discussing it after that and I thought she was wising up and maybe beginning to set me up. I had to get in first.'

No! I screamed in my head. The only words the informant said were, 'It's closer than you think, watch your …' I thought he meant watch my back! I didn't know he meant watch my *husband*! I never suspected you were involved in drug smuggling. I thought you'd just turned into an arsehole of your own accord! You bastard!

'And why Scotty's wife?' Alec demanded. 'She was a druggie; she wasn't any danger to us. You said she was going to rat on us to pay her husband back. But she wasn't, was she? She needed a supplier.'

He looked at the Asian girl and grinned evilly. 'You'd been screwin' her, hadn't you? You got to know her when you were supposed to be defending her in court. And you moved in on her while her old man was in the joint. What happened? Did she threaten to tell Scotty when he got out?'

Paul at least had the good grace to look uncomfortable for a brief moment as he glanced at the Asian girl, who completely ignored the remark and kept the famous inscrutable Asian look on her beautiful face.

'I needed him as a suspect – a decoy or a patsy, if you will,' Paul retorted angrily, 'in case they came to suspect Lucky's accidental death was not what it appeared when *you* cocked up by leaving those signs of a struggle. Scott had trouble with her before when he was arrested for beating up Cheryl. He'd hit Lucky in the struggle and swore he'd get even with her and the other constable who helped make the arrest.'

'Ah, so that's why I had to bash that young guy on the head and throw him in the river when he was fishing.' Alec was receiving a rude awakening as to just how much he'd been used. 'You never told me he was a cop as well. I thought he was a competitor.' He shook his head in disbelief. 'I was just told to follow orders and like a fool I did it without asking the right questions.'

His mind started to add things up. 'So, you had it in for Scotty the whole time? You had the hots for his wife and decided to frame Scotty. How were you going to do that without evidence that Scotty had killed your wife?'

Paul shrugged. 'She and the young cop you hit over the head and drowned had both arrested him and given evidence in court. He was heard to threaten them, he'd just been released from prison, his estranged wife was found drowned in the bath in the same manner, and he absconded. Hasn't been seen since he left prison and therefore he has no alibi, and hasn't reported for his meetings with his parole officer since his release. Circumstantial, but if a good prosecutor couldn't make a case out of that he isn't worth his salt.'

'And what about Scotty? He told me he'd known Cheryl had been fucking another man. He said he could smell another man in the house. That was you, wasn't it? It's that bloody smelly aftershave you wear. So what happens now, an anonymous telephone call to the police informing them where he can be found?'

Paul shrugged again. 'Cologne, not aftershave,' he snarled, superciliously. 'Well, either that or I give you another little chore.'

Alec was disgusted. 'No way. I'm not going to be responsible for killing one of our brothers. *And* I don't care where your bloody scent comes from.'

'Ex-brothers,' Paul reminded him. 'And you're really not in a position to refuse. I've got too much on you, my friend. You also went off on your own bat and killed your football mate, Bruce's ex-girlfriend, remember?'

'I didn't kill her,' Alec almost screamed at him. 'Bruce did. He reckoned he had a better chance of getting into her apartment than I did. He pretended he was going to make up with her and she let him in. He got her pissed and she let him undress her so they could share a bath together. All I did was pretend to be him to fool that nosey neighbour and the poofey manager. We'd made a recording of Bruce and Natasha screaming and moaning like they were fucking and played that back when the two old goats came to the door.'

'That still makes you and Natasha accessories, Alec old boy,' Paul smiled patronisingly.

I had sat in the corner of the office listening intently, astounded and appalled at the revelations. But strangely, it didn't affect me as emotionally as it would have if I had been alive and a serving police officer when I witnessed it. It was more like watching a crime show on television, involved but removed, somehow. And there it was, four cases rolled into one; five if

130

you count Tony's murder; and six if you count the drug dealing, explained if not completely solved to my satisfaction. But how in the name of hell was I going to bring Paul and Alec to justice?

Evelyn was my only chance but there was no way she'd front the police again after her last humiliation.

I was distracted by the Asian woman's voice.

'Besides,' she said, in slightly accented but perfect English, 'my father back in Thailand will be very unhappy if his business is interrupted. And he so looks forward to having Paul visit him to organise the shipping details. He also has a lot at stake. I would not advise you to cross him. He has much experience in dealing with traitors.'

So that was the reason for Paul's constant trips to Thailand, to organise the shipping of the drugs. But how does he do it?

'So I was right all along about Bruce murdering Sheila,' Evelyn said in triumph.

She sat at her kitchen table, scoffing down a bowl of muesli and a couple of million-calorie chocolate croissants and coffee for her health breakfast, followed by a laxative pill as compensation.

'But how did he get out and back in again without being recognised?' I said.

'The coat,' she replied, as if a smart cop like me should've worked it out by now. 'Bruce sneaked out while the manager and Stanley Boucher were confronting Natasha and Alec at the apartment door, went around to Sheila's, convinced her he wanted to make up with her, she let him in, he got her drunk on vodka, seduced her, suggested they share a bath, and voila! One dead ex-girlfriend who had been threatening to expose him for drug taking and probably dealing, if he tried to drop her. That wouldn't look good for a rising football star.'

131

'And Alec sneaked out wearing Bruce's very recognisable overcoat and probably a hat, the next morning with Natasha, supposedly on their way to breakfast.' I began to see another light at the end of another tunnel, so to speak, and I continued, with growing awareness. 'The two men swapped clothes and it was Bruce who returned with Natasha the next morning and was recognised by the manager and Boucher, right?'

'Right on, Ms Dead Detective,' Evelyn replied, daintily dabbing her mouth with her napkin. 'And I'll bet you Alec has kept the CD as insurance or blackmail. All we've got to do is find that and turn it over to the cops somehow.'

I looked at her, imploringly.

'Ah, no,' she said, with finality, 'not in my work description.'

'Maybe it's hidden in their clubroom office?' I tried to sound optimistic. 'Maybe somebody could find an excuse to get in there and have a look around?' I said, outrageously inveigling her. 'Somebody who's a member of the club?'

'Definitely not,' she stated firmly. 'I'm liable to finish up taking a bath with Alec. I've told you for the last time, I'm out.'

Back to the drawing board.

Tony was at the desk next to mine when I returned.

'Tony, how long had you been here before I arrived?'

He looked at me with a puzzled expression. 'Oh, I don't know, time doesn't mean much here.' He went back to his work.

'I was just wondering,' I said, casually. 'You see, from what I've learned, it looks like you didn't just slip and fall in to the river. It seems you were bashed on the head with a rock and thrown into the river to drown.'

His expression turned to one of surprise.

'I honestly don't remember. I just blacked out for a moment and next thing I was up here. I wasn't aware of being bashed.'

'Hmm, interesting, isn't it?'

132

I explained what I'd learned, spying on Paul and Alec, and he was very excited.

'The bastards!' he exclaimed triumphantly. 'Well, that's it, you've got them.'

'Oh yes, I've got them but the police haven't got them and I doubt if they ever will. You see, there's no proof, no evidence. They certainly aren't going to confess and I can't tell the police because they can't hear me, and dear old Evelyn is not in their good books and refuses to give me any more help.'

'Something will turn up, you'll see,' he said, encouragingly. 'Apparently there's a natural justice at work up here; we may not get the result we think we want but it works itself out in the end.'

I only hoped he was right. Paul, Alec, Bruce and Natasha deserved justice and I really wanted them to get it. Was that revenge I felt creeping in? Of course not, I excused myself, it was my need to see justice done.

Evelyn had just had her shower, washed her hair and thrown on a long satin house dress, a midnight blue number with an all-over pattern of shooting stars and planets. Around her head she'd wound a purple towel as a sort of turban.

She had ground the coffee and was waiting for the coffee machine to heat when the front door bell rang. Opening the door, she was confronted by a most unexpected visitor, none other than Homicide Detective Sergeant Howell, looking much more contrite than he had at their previous meeting. He was obviously a little surprised by her appearance, looking as she did in what he considered the perfect outfit for a practising spiritual medium.

'I'm sorry to disturb you, Ms Marsh, but I was wondering if you could spare me a moment or are you busy with a client?'

'What?' Evelyn was somewhat puzzled, and then looked down at her outfit and laughed.

'No, I don't have "clients" anymore, Detective Sergeant. I've just had a shower and thrown on this old housecoat while my hair dries. What can I do for you?'

'Would it be possible for me to come in for a moment?' he asked, a little uncomfortably. 'There's something I would like to discuss with you.'

Puzzled, Evelyn stood back, allowed him to pass in front of her and indicated the living room. He nodded his thanks and rather stiffly entered the room where she invited him to sit.

'I'm just making coffee, can I get you a cup?'

He accepted and sat down on one of the armchairs, looking around the room, somewhat surprised at its normality. Evelyn moved into the kitchen and took a couple of coffee mugs down from a cupboard above the room divider bench.

'Just black, thank you,' he said, unasked. She nodded, wondering about the reason for this unexpected visit.

'Have you seen this morning's paper?' he asked.

'No,' she replied, 'like most people these days I watch the news on tele in the evening, why?'

'They've found the remains of the body of a young boy caught in the reeds near the mouth of the Goulbourn River.'

Evelyn stopped in the middle of pouring the coffee and looked at him. 'James, the young missing boy whose body I said had been moved to a riverbank and probably washed away in the floods?'

He nodded.

She nodded in satisfaction. 'I hate to say I told you so, but I told you so.' She finished pouring the coffees and brought them into the living room, placing one at his side on the small side table.

'There's something else,' he said uncomfortably. 'You were quite right about Bevan being bullied at school by that Sacha boy – and the reason,' he paused, finding it difficult to continue.

134

'I've stopped the affair now and things seem to be returning to normal.'

She nodded, gratified by his confession.

'You'll find Bevan will be much happier now and he'll return to his studies but it may be some time before he forgives you and in the future he will throw it back at you, I'm afraid. But by the time he reaches eighteen he'll understand and eventually forgive you. Your relationship with Bevan will become much stronger as he gets older and knows more about the temptations of the adult world.'

'Is this a private reading?' he smiled.

'That one's a freebie,' she smiled back.

He nodded his thanks. 'I hope you're right.'

He paused for a moment sipping his coffee before looking back at her. 'But the experience made me start thinking about how accurate you had been and then, this morning, when I heard about them finding that young boy's body, well, I started to wonder about what you said regarding Lucky Lambert being murdered and the Sheila Turner case.' He paused and quickly tried to recover his gruffness, 'Of course, I don't believe in all this spiritual malarkey but ... I'd like to go over your theory once again.'

Evelyn looked at him steadily, trying to decide if she was prepared to go on with helping Lucky bring the killers to justice. Once again, she felt she didn't have an option.

'Well, I must warn you we, I mean I, haven't got any real evidence but I'll tell you what I know to be the truth and what you do with it is entirely up to you.'

'Fair enough,' he agreed.

Evelyn related the facts she and Lucky had discovered and told them in such a way that her relationship with her spirit friend wasn't revealed but in a way that presented the facts about Lucky's death, her husband, Paul's, involvement, the apparent murder of Constable Tony Buchanan, Rusty's ex-partner, Bruce, Natasha and Alec's involvement in the murder of Bruce's ex-girlfriend, Sheila Turner, the apparent suicide of Lucy Warner and the disappearance of her husband, Scott, the drug scene at the Rusty Pistons club and the possible arrival of a shipment of illegal drugs in the near future.

Howell sat listening intently, obviously astounded at the breadth of the conspiracy, and took copious notes in the notebook he'd pulled out of his jacket pocket.

'But I repeat,' Evelyn concluded, 'I have absolutely no evidence of any of this and it all came to me through my psychic power, which you and the police have absolutely no faith in, so I'm actually wasting yours and my time.'

'Maybe so,' Howell concurred, 'but I'll certainly look at all these cases again and see what conclusions I can come to. But, as you say, the police force doesn't officially recognise clairvoyancy and unless we have clear evidence we cannot act on it officially.' He shook his head in wonderment. 'I've got to say, though, your statement relating to all these offences is certainly surprising to say the least. You know I can't promise I can act on any of your accusations.'

'I understand, Detective Sergeant,' Evelyn responded cynically. 'That's only as I would expect.'

Chapter 13

That evening, Evelyn had a date with Jason. He'd tentatively asked her if maybe she'd like to have dinner with him, suspecting she would refuse, but was surprised and apparently delighted that she'd accepted. They met at an Italian restaurant in Lygon Street. It wasn't one of the more upmarket restaurants that were prolific in the area but at least it wasn't a McDonald's. Jason ordered a bottle of red and as they sat drinking before the meal arrived, Evelyn once again attempted to dissuade him from taking on the job he'd mentioned that was set for the twenty-seventh of the month.

'It's just not worth it, Jason. That Alec is a very bad bastard and you'd be mad to follow him. I have a very nasty feeling about it and, believe me, my feelings are very seldom wrong.'

'I can't get out of it, Ev,' he said, reluctantly. 'Anyway, I'm only along for the ride in case of trouble from any of the rival gangs that may have heard about it. The competition's pretty strong out there in this line of business – very nasty sometimes.'

'I take it there's a delivery of drugs involved, am I right?' she asked, *sotto vocé*.

Jason didn't respond but by his expression she knew she was right.

'Well, at least let's meet up at the club after you're finished. I just want to know you're alright.'

He considered her proposal.

'Alright, I'll meet you in the upstairs club room at midnight. I'll leave a key buried in the sand in the ashtray on the floor just outside the door.'

Yes! thought Evelyn. I'll get there early and have a chance to case the joint while they're all out on the job. Perfect.

'I don't suppose you'll tell me where the pick-up is?'

He shook his head. 'Too risky. But I can tell you it's in Westernport Bay.'

The intuitive flash again invaded her mind: the water, a boat, a jetty, death.

'Please be careful, Jason, I'm really very worried about you.'

He patted her hand that was resting on the table in front of her and smiled.

'No one's ever been worried about me before. That's very nice.'

On the night of the twenty-seventh, Evelyn arrived at the Rusty Pistons Clubhouse at about ten-thirty. The dinner dance was in full swing with the elderly couples drinking, dancing and consuming the delicious supper that the social committee had graciously provided. She greeted a few of the other members, sipped a glass of wine or two, and eagerly partook of the supper of quiche, sausage rolls, sandwiches, patties, lavish cakes of all varieties and a dish of 'vitamins' which sat in the middle of the laden table. She gave the 'vitamins' a miss but sampled all the other dishes.

After a respectable time spent establishing her presence, she wandered out into the corridor and sneaked up the stairs to the big boys' club. As Jason had promised, he'd left a key hidden in the sand of the ashtray by the door. Covered by the noise of Buddy Holly, Elvis Presley and the Beatles, she slipped the key into the lock and turned it. The lock clicked, she opened the door, entered the smelly outer room and made for the office. Damn, the cupboard door was padlocked! Her talents not running to lock picking she looked around the room for an implement that would help her gain entry.

Meanwhile, I followed Paul from his apartment as he drove his BMW sedan to the St Kilda marina and watched as he made his way along the pier to his 17.6-metre offshore fishing cruiser. It was an aluminium mono hull by the name of *Zebedee*. He'd bought it just after we were married in the better days of our relationship when he was an up-and-coming successful lawyer. We'd had many days' outings on board and a few romantic nights on the ten-berth boat where he treated me like a queen with French champagne and suppers to die for, which eventually, of course, I did.

Where had I gone wrong? We were in love, I thought. We had a bright future ahead of us, he was getting very influential clients and the money was rolling in. Little did I know then, some of those clients were organised crime bosses who expected value for their patronage. I also hadn't realised that he had become addicted to the money and the power he possessed whilst becoming indebted to the crime syndicates.

I had almost given up my career for him as a cop but I was also ambitious and despite his urging I had insisted on continuing with my career. I realised now why he was so insistent. Although it could be useful with his wife being a detective it was also a danger that I might inadvertently discover his criminal involvement. That's where it all went wrong. But to lead him to the point where he actually arranged for my demise was unforgivable, even now in the afterlife. I obviously had a long way to go to find forgiveness. Another test?

Paul met a couple of boat owners on the pier and exchanged pleasantries, saying he was going out for a night's fishing. They wished him well as he jumped aboard, checked that the three-metre aluminium dinghy with the attached outboard motor he towed was secured and started the *Zebedee*'s powerful motor. Slowly he pulled away from the marina berth and out into the river, exited at the Port of Melbourne and sailed out into the ocean, heading west.

I floated above the boat remembering the joy I had experienced in the old days when he would open up the throttle and the boat would plane and we'd cut through the waves and across the surface like we were flying. Well, now I was, and it was even better.

Suddenly I noticed he was not alone on the deck; a passenger had appeared from the cabin and joined him. It was Alec! He'd obviously been hiding away in one of the sleeping cabins by pre-arrangement because Paul didn't appear surprised to see him. Paul opened up the throttle and the boat roared out to sea. The two men stood side by side their eyes glued to the distance. After a few miles and well into the shipping lane, Paul closed the throttle and the boat slowed to a crawl. Both men had picked up night vision binoculars and were looking over the side intently. Suddenly I saw Paul point to the starboard side and heard him say, 'There it is!' He adjusted the steering and Alec picked up a long-handled fish gaff. The boat drifted to a stop beside a red marker and Alec leaned over the side and with the gaff hook snared the rope connected to the marker and pulled it in.

On the end of the rope was a large plastic-wrapped bag. Ah, the drugs! I thought. So that's how they do it. The drugs are thrown overboard from a cargo ship or container at a predetermined location and time, and Paul and Alec retrieve them. Not a very original idea but an effective one. There must be tons of drugs smuggled into the country from the East in this manner and it's very hard to locate them without information and good intelligence.

Suddenly I had a premonition of what was about to happen. There was absolutely nothing I could do about it but let the saga play out to its destiny.

Paul turned the boat towards shore and a small, private, obscured jetty, where Jason was waiting. This was where Paul would drop Alec off to take the drugs they had retrieved back to their clubhouse or some other safe location. Just before they reached the jetty, I saw Alec pick up the long-handled fish gaff and take a few steps to stand behind Paul who was intent on steering the boat through the patches of sea grass that were beginning to appear from the shoreline. He raised the gaff high and swung it down savagely on Paul's head. The blow struck Paul squarely on the side of his head, sending him sprawling and unconscious, or dead, onto the deck of the *Zebedee*. Alec stood over his body with a triumphant sneer on his face.

'Your blue-collar worker has just been promoted, arsehole. Now it's my turn to run the show.'

He set the motor into idle and bent to drag Paul's body to the rail. With difficulty he pushed it over the side into the dark water where it floated face down and unmoving. Satisfied he had exacted his revenge, he quickly transferred the drugs into the dinghy attached to the stern of the *Zebedee*, grabbed a spare fuel tank standing nearby, undid the cap and splashed the fuel over the deck, then threw the near-empty can into the cabin. He pulled the dinghy to the side of the trawler, climbed in and picked up a handful of fuel-soaked rags he had prepared earlier, lit them with a cigarette lighter from his jacket pocket and threw the burning torch into the *Zebedee*. The spilt fuel ignited and immediately burst into flames.

Suddenly there was the sound of water police sirens bearing down on the scene from nearby. Alec reacted to the imminent danger, gunned the outboard motor of the aluminium dinghy and sped off as close to the shore as possible in an easterly direction as fast as the outboard would allow. The water police arrived at the scene of the burning boat and immediately attempted to

141

douse the flames but the fire had taken control and their efforts were wasted. In no time the *Zebedee* was virtually destroyed.

They dragged Paul's lifeless body from the water and laid it on their deck.

Well, I thought, Alec had done it again. He'd obviously hidden away in the *Zebedee* at the St Kilda marina, on Paul's instruction and unseen by any possible observers. They would then retrieve the drugs and hand them over to the bikie gang members on shore at a previously arranged spot and Paul could return alone to the marina and establish his alibi if necessary with other boat owners who happened to be in dock. But as Alec hadn't been seen at the marina it also gave him an alibi to dispose of his hated boss and take over the drug operation. Paul would be found floating in the bay, near his burnt-out boat, obviously a terrible fishing accident; once again a crime with no obvious evidence. It was ironic that Paul had met his death in basically the same way that he had caused me to meet mine, bashed over the head and drowned.

I watched as Paul's spirit slowly detached itself from his body and floated just above the surface of the water where it was joined by several murky grey wraiths who appeared to lift him as they all rose into the night sky and disappeared. I don't know if he was transported into another dimension but I could no longer see them. I had a strong instinct that Paul's spirit was following my journey through the tunnel into the afterlife but when it came to the junction of the light and the dark sides I felt I knew in which direction he would be taken. Was this an example of the Universal justice Tony had talked about?

Alec, hidden by the dense mangroves, manoeuvred his little dinghy into another secret jetty a few kilometres from the spot where the *Zebedee* and Paul had met their fate. Ruffo and Pete, his two usual accomplices, were waiting for him. The drugs

142

package was silently transferred to Ruffo's saddlebag, Alec climbed on the pillion seat and the three men steered their two bikes along the narrow path through the mangroves to the main road.

Evelyn quickly returned to her scooter in the car park of the Rusty Pistons Club, dug into her tool kit, selected a thin, metal tyre lever and a hammer, and returned upstairs to the office where she jemmied the door. She inserted the tyre lever into the padlock on the cupboard and after a deal of effort with the hammer, the lock snapped open. Laying the lever and hammer on the desk she investigated the contents of the cupboard and found a stack of bank notes in bundles, a red notebook that recorded the criminal activities of the gang, and a flat cigar box that contained a Yale key. And yes, there it was: a CD which she was certain was the recording of Bruce and Natasha's sexual romp that Stanley Boucher and Mr Bright heard the night Bruce was out killing Sheila Turner. What an absolute treasure trove!

She slipped the CD and key into her coat pocket and was wondering where she could conceal the notebook when the answer suddenly occurred to her: in her knickers. Nobody was likely to be getting into her knickers that night judging from her recent history. But at that moment, with her skirt up around her waist, Jason suddenly stepped into the room.

She had her back to him but it was obvious to him her skirt was lifted above her waist revealing her baggy pink nylon bloomers.

'Well,' he said, 'I was only expecting a chat and maybe a drink or two but I see you have something else on your mind.'

She spun around in surprise, trying to adjust her clothing. 'Jason! You're earlier than I expected. Thank God you're alright. What happened?'

He was obviously upset and tense but attempted to cover it. 'Mac and I went to the spot Alec told me to but he never showed up. But the cops did. They wanted to know what we were doing there and I told them I was checking out our crab pots. They told us to piss off as they were conducting a stakeout. They'd obviously had a tip-off. It wasn't you, was it?' he asked suspiciously.

'How could it be? I didn't know where you were going.'

'I told you I was going to Westernport Bay.'

'That's a pretty big area, Jason. You never pinpointed exactly where you were going.'

'Yeah, that's true,' he admitted.

Suddenly Evelyn heard my urgent warning in her head.

'Evelyn, Alec's on his way upstairs!'

'Shit!' she said, quickly closing the cupboard door and grabbing Jason by his jacket collar and pulling him into a passionate embrace with her back leaning on the cupboard door.

Alec entered carrying the pack of drugs and stopped dead in his tracks, staring at Evelyn and Jason in what appeared to be a raunchy, sexual embrace.

'What the hell,' he said angrily. 'What are you two doing up here?'

They both spun around guiltily.

'This is not your own private fucking den, Jason. And how the fuck did you get in here?'

'Sorry, Alec,' Jason replied, awkwardly. 'I just got here and thought you'd arrived back. But I found Pixie outside waiting for me. The office door was open and well, it was obvious what she had on her mind so,' he paused, improvising frantically, 'well, at my age I can't afford to let an opportunity go by, can I?'

'Piss off and get the fuck out of here,' Alec ordered.

144

'Where did you get to, Alec?' Jason asked, trying to distract Alec's attention, 'We waited where you told us but you never showed up.'

'I had to change my plans,' Alec replied gruffly dismissing them. 'So get out of here.'

It was then Alec noticed the tyre lever and hammer on the desk where Evelyn had placed them while she ransacked the cupboard. His eyes flew to the cupboard and immediately noticed the broken padlock.

'Hold it right there,' he said as he removed a lethal looking handgun from his coat pocket and pointed it at the pair. 'Who busted the padlock?'

Jason and Evelyn shared a terrified look and attempted to look innocent.

'It was open when we came in,' Evelyn lied, unconvincingly.

'Oh, no it wasn't,' Alec answered threateningly, as he walked towards them with the pistol raised. 'I made damn sure it was locked when I left.' He picked up the tyre lever. 'The lock's been jemmied,' he said. He looked at each of them in turn and then gestured with the gun to Evelyn. Obviously Jason wouldn't have had the time to break in and smash the padlock having just arrived back from Westernport Bay. She nervously stepped toward him and stopped. With his spare hand he quickly frisked her coat pockets but found nothing to enlighten him. He began to run his hand over the rest of her body but as he reached her waist she screamed as if being violated and stepped back.

'I didn't take anything!' she wailed desperately. 'I passed a couple in the hall as I arrived up here to meet Jason,' she improvised spontaneously. 'Maybe they broke in. I think it was Valerie and Bob,' she blurted out suspecting they must know something about the drug association seeing they were obviously supplying the amphetamines to the elderly members and could have broken in to boost their stocks.

145

Alec would never find out for sure because at that moment Detective Sergeant Howell and three police officers, dressed in riot gear, with weapons at the ready, pushed Evelyn and Jason out of the way and stormed the office, screaming 'Police! Down on the floor! Don't move!' Alec reacted immediately and fired a shot but it went astray as Evelyn quickly snatched the tyre lever and smashed it against Alec's hand. She amazed herself at the speed in which she had reacted. He screamed and dropped the gun and there was a violent scuffle but he was quickly overpowered by the officers who held and handcuffed him.

'You were under surveillance from the moment you and Paul Lambert left the marina, my friend, both by helicopter, radar and infrared. I have to admit,' he smiled sardonically, 'I didn't expect you to set fire to the boat and that sort of strained our resources and delayed us for a bit. Paul Lambert's body was found floating nearby. Have a little disagreement, did we?'

'Fuck off,' Alec responded, angrily.

Howell turned his back to Alec and gave Evelyn a knowing wink. Alec glared at Jason, suspecting he had informed on him but Jason gave an innocent shrug of ignorance of any betrayal.

My God, thought Evelyn, he killed Lucky's ex-husband! Well, there's justice for you. The bastard certainly had it coming to him. They could never prove that he'd had Lucky murdered but he didn't get away with it in the end.

'You had us worried when you didn't land where we expected you to and we lost you there for a minute but I suspected this is where you'd end up and the radar and infrared did the rest. We got your two mates downstairs too, by the way. They're singing their hearts out. They didn't know murder was a part of your plan but whether they like it or not they'll be considered accomplices. As for you,' he turned to Jason but Evelyn jumped in to protect him.

'No, officer, he was with me here for most of the evening.'

146

Howell went to disagree with her but she gave him a sly wink and he made no further comment.

Alec, his two accomplices and the drugs were taken away to the awaiting patrol cars and Howell turned to Evelyn with a conspiratorial smile.

'You two are missing out on the dinner dance downstairs. It sounds like they're having a ball so why don't you join them. I'll drop down myself in a minute and maybe have a bite of supper and a coffee. There's just a few things up here I have to clean up.'

The police raid hadn't gone unnoticed by the revellers at the dinner dance who streamed outside to catch the drama as it unfolded. This was the most action any of them had seen since Vietnam, Korea or possibly even the Second World War for some of them and there was great excitement. But after a few minutes they filed back into their clubroom, chatting excitedly, and the party continued.

As Jason and Evelyn grabbed a bite of supper, Evelyn noticed the bowl of 'multivitamins' had mysteriously disappeared from the centre of the supper table and Valerie and Bob had quietly disappeared.

After downing a cold beer, Jason invited Evelyn to join him on the dance floor, which she happily accepted.

'Thanks for the alibi, Ev,' he whispered in her ear and she responded with a smile.

'I warned you not to go there tonight but you didn't listen. Anyway, you weren't involved in any crime so I couldn't see you arrested with those bastards.'

'I think Alec was only using me as a decoy. He never intended meeting up with me; he'd planned to go straight to the other two in the first place and leave me to deal with any opposition.' He looked at her with a cheeky grin. 'So you *are* some kind of psychic?' he said jokingly.

She laughed. 'You ought to see what I can do with my crystal ball and wand – Harry Potter, eat your heart out.'

'I can't wait,' he laughed.

After only a couple of minutes of rocking away to an Elvis Presley classic, Detective Sergeant Howell joined them on the dance floor and asked Jason if he'd mind if he cut in. Jason agreed readily and moved on to partner Desley who had been waltzing with Jack, quite oblivious to the rock 'n roll beat.

'Well,' said Howell, as he led Evelyn to one side of the dance floor, 'thanks for the phone call warning us about tonight. It looks like we might have tied up the whole mess, thanks to you.'

'I can't tell you how glad I was when you broke in and saved me up there,' she said, gratefully. 'After our last conversation I didn't know if you'd take any notice of me.'

'I didn't say anything to Superintendent Blake. You know what his reaction would have been. But I got to thinking about all your claims and did a bit of sniffing around, just to check you out. After all, you did come up with a few surprising facts about me which you couldn't know about,' he said with a slight flush. 'I had Paul Lambert investigated and found he had links to some of the organised crime bosses when he'd acted for them in a few cases, and that made me a bit suspicious. I then found he had a boat, the *Zebedee*, and with your input, I started to put two and two together. We put a tail on him tonight just in case your predictions were right, and they were.

'I also checked out Alec Sanderland who had previous on suspected drug dealing, and Lambert managed to get him off. I also found his connection to the unlikely Rusty Pistons Motorcycle Club, which was supposedly an over-fifties social club. There's often a secret, separate outlaw division in these clubs but we'd never established it as a fact with the Rusty

Pistons. I told Blake I'd had a hot tip from one of my informants about a possible drug pick-up and he approved the operation after a lot of talking. He'll be thrilled with the outcome. I didn't mention your name, of course.'

Evelyn nodded her thanks. 'And what about Cheryl Warner? Paul was having an affair with her while her husband was in prison and I'm sure Alec drowned her in the bath on Paul's orders when she threatened him and laid the blame on her husband, Scott. Scott Warner was supposed to be the patsy for Paul Lambert and Alec in case things got nasty for them.'

He held up his hand to interrupt her. 'We'll look into that if and when we find her husband.'

'Oh, I can help you out there,' she said confidentially. 'He's hiding out in a winery up near Shepparton.'

He looked at her, astounded. 'How the hell do you know that? No, don't tell me, another of your psychic moments?'

She gave him a non-committal smile and he shook his head in amazed disbelief.

'And what about Bruce Curlew and his girlfriend, Natasha?' she asked.

'We're looking into that too. We'll run forensic tests on Bruce Curlew's coat and see if we can pick up any of Alec's DNA. I wish we could find that audio disc you were talking about, if one exists.'

She suddenly remembered. 'Oh, I think it does.' She looked around and saw Jason's coat lying across one of the chairs nearby. 'Hang on.' She picked up the coat, searched one of the pockets and pulled out the CD she'd discovered in the upstairs office. She handed it to Howell who looked at it in further amazement.

'I slipped this into Jason's pocket while I was pashing on with him before Alec arrived on the scene.'

149

He looked at her in bewilderment, not daring to ask about her and Jason's relationship in case she went into more lurid detail.

'Don't ask,' she responded.

'Where did you find this disc?' he asked incredulously.

'Upstairs in Alec's office cupboard,' she replied smugly. 'And oh yes, there's this.' She turned her back on Howell, lifted her skirt, fished around in her panties and withdrew the red notebook she'd also found. 'This might help, also. I doubt he'd run the risk of putting the details on his computer in case you lot raided them sometime.'

He took the book in astonishment and opened it. 'Anything else you've got stashed away down there?'

'Nothing you're going to see,' she replied coquettishly. 'No, I think that's the lot.' She patted herself down to make sure. 'Oh, wait a minute, there's this key. I think you may find it fits your comrade, Lucky Lambert's apartment door. I think Paul Lambert had a copy made and gave it to Alec so he could break in and drown her. He was Paul's hit man, you see.'

'You mean her death wasn't accidental?' he asked incredulously. She shook her head in the negative.

By now Howell was past amazement and simply stared at her.

'All this explaining has made me a little peckish,' she said with an impish grin. 'I think I'll just check out the supper table again. Care to join me?'

He declined, saying he had to get back to the station and sort things out. But he stood, still a little overcome by her revelations.

'I say, I don't suppose you'd be interested in joining the force, would you?' he asked rather cynically.

She turned with a self-deprecating smile. 'Oh, I don't think so. The police force doesn't believe in psychics, do they? And besides, this will definitely be my last case. I think I'll go back to telling middle-aged ladies about winning the lottery, their daughter's weddings and a dark stranger with a throbbing penis entering their life. You gotta give people hope.'

I floated up near the ceiling watching. Evelyn had certainly accomplished her task and more. She'd also helped me clear up nearly all my outstanding cases and a few I didn't know existed. We'd made a good team, I thought, and I was determined to keep in touch with her in the future.

Howell left like a man on a mission and Evelyn and Jason resumed dancing, this time to a romantic ballad by Frank Sinatra.

I floated over to them and said, 'Evelyn, you've been absolutely brilliant, thank you so much.'

She opened her eyes and looked at me dreamily over Jason's shoulder.

'Piss off, Lucky,' she whispered.

Chapter 14

I had decided to give Evelyn a bit of her own space for a while and we'd had no contact for a few weeks of Earth time. Besides, I had things to learn about my new situation. I attended instruction sessions with Joseph who appeared in many guises but I had the certainty that they were all aspects of him. I also had what I referred to as my 'rest periods' or 'end-of-term holidays', where I could contemplate the lessons I had learned and the mistaken beliefs I had formulated whilst being held to the attachments I had formed during my incarnations on the Earth plane. It was wonderfully gentle and constructive and my knowledge of the seemingly endless levels or dimensions grew.

Evelyn was back to her gardening and seemingly more peaceful with herself when her doorbell rang. On the doorstep was Homicide Detective Senior Sergeant Howell, smiling and eager to relate the further developments that had eventuated in his investigations. She invited him to join her in the back courtyard.

'We reopened the Sheila Turner case,' he almost beamed, 'and you'll be pleased to know we sent Bruce Curlew's overcoat off to forensics and got a positive result of Alec Sanderland's DNA. He'd definitely been wearing it but he claimed it had obviously happened when he borrowed the coat from Bruce Curlew sometime. But the CD was just too much of a coincidence. You were right, it was exactly what Stanley Boucher and Mr Bright had heard when they confronted who they thought was Bruce and Natasha. They altered their statements to say they thought they recognised Curlew by his voice but neither could definitely identify him as they only had a quick glimpse of his bare body and the back of his head. Alec denies it of course, but with all the other evidence I'd say we have a bloody good chance of getting him for the lot.'

'And what about Lucky and Paul Lambert's murders?' Evelyn asked. 'And Lucy Warner's?'

Howell looked doubtful. 'That's going to be more difficult because there were absolutely no eye witnesses to the actual killings and, so far, only circumstantial and no admissible evidence. But I'm not giving up hope yet. The Prosecution lawyers are working on it. The investigation is ongoing. But one thing's for sure, he'll go away for a long time and Paul Lambert's paid for his involvement anyway.'

'And Scott Warner?' Evelyn asked.

'We raided the winery and found the drug stash. Nunzio Vertoli's been arrested but there was no sign of Warner.'

Evelyn had a quick intuitive flash of Scott in far north Queensland, sitting in a pub with a cold beer and looking out over the ocean. His appearance had changed drastically with the help of plastic surgery and a new identity. Well, she thought, he hadn't really committed any crime since he'd been out of prison, so good luck to him.

Howell paused thoughtfully and looked a little uncomfortable as he finally mentioned what he'd really come to talk about with Evelyn.

'Evelyn,' he said cautiously.

'Yes, Derek,' she smiled, returning the compliment of his informality.

'The remains of that young boy we found at the mouth of the Goulbourn.'

Evelyn's face fell into an expression of extreme sadness. 'James?'

Howell nodded. 'We've reopened the case.' He paused again. 'I took soil samples from the location where you said he was originally buried. They matched with samples found in the boy's mouth during the autopsy.'

She nodded. Although her information had been justified, she was still left with a dreadful sadness for the boy and his parents; a feeling of unfinished business with the killer still being free, hung over her.

'Would you be prepared to help us out again? Not officially, of course,' he added quickly. 'But now I know what you're capable of, maybe you can come up with something. I mean with this sort of an apparently random case, we have very little to go on.'

She had a strong inclination not to involve herself again in the case that had originally turned her away from using her psychic talents. She stood and, needing time to consider the implications of once again hurting the parents, she offered her usual method of delaying a decision.

'Coffee?' she asked, moving towards the kitchen.

'Great,' he replied.

'Black, right?' she asked brightly.

He nodded as she disappeared out of sight and waited for her reply to his request. He could hear her filling the kettle and preparing the cups.

She re-emerged from the kitchen and sat opposite him on one of the patio chairs.

'I don't really see how much more help I could be,' she said. 'But if you promise my name will not be brought into it and this is just kept between us, then alright, I'll do what I can.'

He breathed a sigh of relief and smiled.

'Thanks, Evelyn, and I promise your name will be kept right out of it.'

'Even with Blake?' she replied with a smile.

'Especially with Blake,' he smiled back.

'Evelyn here again! Get your skinny little arse down here again ASAP!'

Surprised at the forceful instruction, I immediately flew down to join her. I was getting pretty good at this by now and was eager to find out the cause of the command.

'Right,' she said as I settled myself down on the sofa. 'I've helped you out and put myself in extreme danger in doing so, I might add,' she said, in a solemn and one could say, demanding manner. 'Now it's your turn to help me.'

'Anything,' I assured her. 'Just say the word.'

'Howell's re-opening the case of Jamie, the young boy who disappeared two years ago and whose remains were found at the mouth of the Goulbourn River a little while back.'

'I remember that case,' I said. 'It's never been solved. Wasn't there something to do with the parents hiring a medium to find out what happened to him? I remember nothing came of it and there was a lot of bad press about it.' I suddenly remembered Evelyn's biography that I'd read on the web that stated she was the medium involved. 'Oh,' I said. 'Sorry, that was you, wasn't it?'

In our own ways we both shared an embarrassing moment.

'Yes, well,' she said, quietly, 'I never got over that because when the police went to the spot I indicated I suddenly got a flash that the body had been moved. I tried to explain it to the police who were digging but they ridiculed me as just another fake medium trying to make a name for herself and any further involvement on my side was definitely unwelcome. I tried to tell them the body had been moved to the side of a creek or a river but of course they wouldn't listen to me; couldn't really blame them, of course.'

I sent sympathy and love out to her but she shrugged it off.

'Anyway,' she said, recovering herself a little, 'they've now found the remains stuck in some reeds or weeds at the mouth of the Goulbourn River. I tried to tell Blake they'd probably been washed down river in the floods but he dismissed me when he read about my involvement in the files on the case.'

'I remember,' I said. 'I was the cause of your Tourettes attack that day, remember?'

She laughed half-heartedly, remembering how she had reacted. 'Anyway, now that Howell's more inclined to take me a bit more seriously, he's asked, off the record of course, if I will try and help find young Jamie's killer. I don't really know what more I can do,' she said hopelessly. 'All I saw was the man kidnapping Jamie and that he was in a white van and I saw him burying the body. I didn't see his face but I saw he was wearing khaki overalls and dirty boots; that's all.'

I thought for a moment and then said, 'Why don't we take a trip out to the original spot and see if something else stirs up a vision? It might be stronger with the two of us there – you know, double the power.'

She looked at me doubtfully trying to see my logic which I admit even eluded me, but she nodded.

'On one condition, you'll have to ride with me on the back of the scooter. You'd be able to get there in the blink of an eye and I'm not going all that way again by myself.'

'Deal,' I said.

Even being in spirit I was terrified riding on the back of the scooter with Evelyn's rather erratic driving. It was not an experience for the faint of heart. She had the knack of driving in the middle of the road and pushing the speed to the limit, missing oncoming cars and trucks by centimetres, speeding through orange traffic lights, taking corners sharply and only occasionally remembering to use her indicators. I tried to close my eyes but that didn't seem to help as I could still see everything. To the accompaniment of blaring horns and the angry abuse of other drivers who dared to presume they had any right on her road, we finally made our way out of the city heading for Warrandyte and into the relative quiet of the outer suburbs, which only encouraged Evelyn to increase her speed. So focused was she that only occasionally did she shout a few words over her shoulder to me, which must have looked to other drivers like she was screaming to herself or at them and therefore quite mad and a fellow road user to avoid at all cost.

We eventually arrived at our destination, which was a rocky, bushy area accessed by a dirt track. I remembered the area around Warrandyte had been a gold rush area in the late eighteen hundreds and I had seen evidence of ancient fossicking sites along the way. This area was never as large as the Ballarat or Bendigo fields but had attracted its share of diggers. I floated off the back of the scooter in great relief and settled next to her as she dismounted. We took a few moments to adjust and get our bearings and then she pointed to the spot where the young boy had initially been buried.

Despite the printed warning not to dump rubbish, people had obviously continued to ignore the restriction with the result that there was a heap of lawn clippings, garden refuse, rusty or worn-out washing machines and stoves and other household appliances, cardboard boxes and bundles of papers, bits of metal and wood and all sorts of smelly and dilapidated junk. Nearby, stood an abandoned council bulldozer that obviously wasn't keeping up with supply.

'Hasn't changed much in a couple of years,' Evelyn said, 'except there's more of it.' She walked past the edge of the dump and pointed to a spot under a scraggly tree. 'There,' she said, 'that's where he buried the body.'

We stood on the spot and tried desperately to concentrate our efforts. Occasionally we'd sneak a look at the other to see if any messages were coming through but to no avail. Evelyn would shake her head occasionally as if trying to clear her thoughts and a puzzled look came over her face. She even tried sitting in a lotus position directly on the spot and meditating. After a few minutes she gave up and rose awkwardly to her feet.

'Nothing else, just the same as I got before.' She paused. 'Still very distressing though. Waste of time.' And as an afterthought she added, 'Don't know what's happening; Angela's not coming through or if she's trying I'm not getting anything from her. She must be pissed off with me for cutting her out.'

She wandered dolefully back to the scooter and replaced her helmet. Where else can we get help? I thought, and then it suddenly occurred to me. I stood on the same spot and focused on Joseph.

'Joseph,' I prayed. Yes, I actually felt as if I was praying. 'We really need your help down here. How about a clue?'

Suddenly I heard his voice in my head.

'Council.'

Chapter 15

The next morning Evelyn rang Derek Howell on the mobile number he had given her.

'Not much luck I'm afraid, Derek,' she said. 'We, I mean I, went back out to the site but I only came up with the same thing: the man was in his late twenties, early thirties, wearing khaki overalls and dirty boots. Oh, and there were some initials or something on the pocket of his overalls, in yellow – MCC it looked like. Oh, and I did get the word "council" but I don't know if he was a councillor or what it meant. Not much help, I'm afraid.'

There was a pause and she could hear the clicking of computer keys on the other end of the line.

'MCC? You never mentioned that before.'

'Didn't I? I'm sure I must have.'

'I'm reading your original statement and there's no mention of an MCC on his pocket.'

'That's strange,' she replied. 'I'd swear I would've mentioned it before. What could it mean?'

'Manningham City Council,' he said, with an edge of excitement creeping into his voice.

'But couldn't that mean Melbourne City Council or the Melbourne Cricket Club?'

'Not in that area,' he replied. 'Manningham City Council covers the Warrandyte area and you said there was a council bulldozer near the site.' His voice now became very excited. 'Suppose the killer dumped the body near where he'd been working, because it was familiar territory, knowing there was little chance of it being found and where he could keep an eye on

159

it, and order people out of the area because dumping rubbish there is prohibited.'

Evelyn began to catch the rising excitement in his voice and her mind went into overdrive.

'But why would he move the body?'

'I don't know. Maybe he was leaving the job and maybe he got scared and thought it might be discovered after he left and he might be implicated, having worked so close to the site, so he decided to move it further away.'

'So it could be of help?'

'Most definitely,' Howell replied, eagerly. 'We can run a check on council workers employed at that time and if nothing comes up we can check the Melbourne City Council and the Melbourne Cricket Club groundsmen. But you did say you got the word council.' He sighed in satisfaction. 'Thanks, Evelyn,' he said warmly. 'You're a genius. You've given us our first real clue. I'll be in touch.'

He hung up and Evelyn stood for a moment holding the phone in her shaking hand while the enormity of the moment sank in. For the first time in the case she was vindicated and gratified that she may have been of some help. Now it was up to the police.

She immediately summoned me. 'Evelyn here, Lucky. Get your clever little arse down here. Great news.'

After Evelyn had explained about her call to Howell, I decided I'd follow him, just to keep an eye on how he was handling the investigation.

He was fast and did everything according to regulations. He immediately contacted the Manningham City Council and was given a list of names of the workers who were employed at the time of the murder. One of the many names that fitted the description and the time was a Brendon Lattimer. Twenty-nine years old, unmarried and an itinerant worker employed as an earth-moving contractor and mainly worked on road construction. But he could have been employed as a rubbish mover. He had finished his contract six months after the murder and moved interstate. It was believed he moved to Western Australia to work in the mines.

Through the Western Australian Police headquarters, Howell circulated Lattimer's name and description to the various mining companies inquiring about his possible recruitment around the time of his disappearance from Victoria, as well as the case background.

Within a short time he received a fax reply through WA Mining stating that, although there was no record of anyone of that name, there was a man of a similar age and description who had arrived in Western Australia from Victoria who had recently been involved in the case of an attempted kidnapping of a young boy but had been released for lack of evidence. Investigations were continuing. A photograph of the suspect was attached. His name was now William Piggs.

Howell immediately took the photograph to Evelyn and the moment she looked at it and laid her hands on it she said, 'That's him, Derek! He's the one!'

Howell immediately notified the WA police that Piggs was now a person of interest and asked if they could detain him on suspicion of murder. They agreed and Howell took the first flight to Perth. I followed him and arrived before his flight even touched down. Clutching his overnight bag, he went directly to Perth's police headquarters, identified himself and asked to interview the suspect.

Piggs, or Lattimer, sat disconsolately in the interview room, his face a mask of fear. He was a good-looking man with dyed blond hair and a muscular build, which was obviously a result of many hours spent in the gym.

161

I studied him before Howell entered and felt it was so sad that a man could sink into such depravity. What had caused this degeneracy? Could it be that no matter how much supposed social acceptance of homosexuality there was, there could never be real inner acceptance by Australian males, as deep down it insulted their masculinity and they found the 'unnatural' attraction abhorrent to them. It may be becoming socially acceptable but I doubted if it would ever become morally acceptable behaviour. If only people had become more enlightened and tolerant earlier on, this crime and many others of a similar vein may have been avoided. But they would rightly never accept these hideous crimes against vulnerable children.

Howell entered escorted by another officer and went through the usual preliminaries. He then began questioning the young man and almost immediately the man began to tremble in fear. When Howell told him that they had received DNA evidence from the boy's body, which in fact was not true, and asked for permission to take a DNA sample for comparison, the young man broke down and collapsed in tears. In a burst of sobbing, he confessed to the crime.

'Yes, alright, I killed the boy!' he screamed in a torrent of mortification. 'I'm so glad it's over,' he blubbered, 'it's been two years of absolute hell and I can't cope with the guilt any longer. I didn't mean it to happen; I just wanted to be with the boy. He shouldn't have screamed and struggled. I wouldn't have hurt him. He shouldn't have screamed and struggled,' he kept repeating, with tears streaming down his face.

'What did you expect him to do? He was eleven years old,' Howell said in disgust.

Chapter 16

I reluctantly returned to my desk and there was Tony and my father chatting away like they'd known each other for years.

'Hi kiddo,' Dad said. 'You know, this is the young man you should've married,' referring to Tony, 'you could've watched each other's backs and neither of you would've ended up here so early.'

I'd swear Tony blushed and I smiled at him.

'Maybe next time around, Dad.'

Either they both disappeared or I was suddenly transported onto another level or dimension because in front of me appeared Joseph, looking as gorgeous as I'd first seen him.

'Mission accomplished,' he said with that disarming smile. 'Congratulations.'

'Thank you,' I said, 'but I have a very strong feeling I had a lot of help.'

'Oh, you did, but that's a part of the test, the journey. You cleaned up nearly all of your outstanding cases; in fact there was another one you didn't know you were instrumental in.'

'Which one was that?' I asked, trying to remember what I'd missed.

'The twins you had arrested for robbery and you knew one of them was a killer but couldn't discover which one it was.'

'Oh, that,' I said, remembering the case Tony and I had discussed.

'They were the two men who were Alec's accomplices, Pete and Ruffo,' he said.

'But,' I said, remembering the two bikies who'd ridden with Alec, 'one was a curly redhead with a bushy beard and moustache and the other had a shaved head like a skinhead.' The light dawned. 'Ah, right, disguises,' I said quite needlessly, 'they changed their MO.'

He nodded. 'They were arrested with Alec and charged as accomplices.'

'Well, what d'you know,' I exclaimed.

'They needed to be caught and given the chance to rehabilitate, which they will, eventually.'

'Well, if you say so,' I said doubtfully. 'By the way, thanks for the tip about that young boy's murder. It eventually cleared up the case. Evelyn is thrilled that her vision was vindicated. She has her self-respect back.'

He nodded. 'And that's another story. But even more importantly, you passed your test and brought Evelyn back into the fold. She was very valuable to us. She provided a lot of help to us over the years of this incarnation but she chose to deny her talents and turn away from the path she originally chose for herself. She was a voice from beyond earthly realms and we need help like that. We can't do it all, you know, we sometimes need people to intercede for us to get things moving. Sometimes people don't even know they're being used and put it down to intuition but that doesn't matter as long as we give them the opportunity.'

'And I was a part of that opportunity?'

He smiled and nodded which again made me think, God, he is a hottie!

'And another strange thing,' I said before he had time to react to my previous thought. 'Evelyn said she's no longer able to call on her guide, Angela, for help – why is that?'

He paused before replying. 'Angela has chosen to move into a different dimension and she has to be replaced as Evelyn's guide.'

'So who's it going to be,' I asked innocently.

He merely smiled again but this time with a knowing look.

'Oh, no,' I said in astonishment as the realisation sank in. 'Do you mean …?

He nodded. 'You're higher up the development level than you imagine. We think you'll make an excellent team. We have also decided that you're ready and highly suitable for the job. If you want it, of course.'

'So, what happens if I say no?' I asked him.

'That all depends on you,' he replied. 'You may choose to stay as you are and keep on working as you have or you may move onto a different level and prepare for another reincarnation and when you're suitably developed, there are many other dimensions to experience. There's no hurry, you know; you have all eternity to decide where you feel you should go next. It's one great adventure and life on Earth is only one aspect of that experience.'

I thought about it for some time and suddenly my decision was clear. I was happy up here, I had no close ties back on Earth, apart from Evelyn, and now I could always get in touch with her, we'd be in constant communication. I wasn't sure how she'd feel about that. My mother would continue on her way until it was time to join us but I'd cope with that then. I still had a long way to go.

'I think I'd like to stay working as I have been, Joseph, with Evelyn if she'll have me. The world is full of crime and it probably always will be considering the frailty of human nature, and the authorities often have their hands tied in bureaucracy and regulations. If we can help out in some way I think that's where I belong for the moment.

'Good choice,' he said.

He smiled and an instant later I was back at my now familiar desk. Tony and the other officers appeared and I recognised some of my colleagues from the past had joined us. I'd better check in with Evelyn and break the news, I thought, and immediately I was transported to the now familiar location.

She and Jason were sitting on the couch. They were kissing passionately and obviously lost in the moment.

'Excuse me, Evelyn,' I said quietly, not wanting to interfere in her ardour but feeling I should tell her of the latest developments.

She broke from the embrace and glanced up at me.

'Piss off, Lucky,' she murmured and immediately returned to the task in hand.

The End

Bryon Williams, ex-stage and television actor, script writer, producer, director turned novelist, has now retired to a Retirement Village in Brisbane. Two of his previous novels, *The Grumpy Old Withered of Oz*, a comedic, semi-autobiographical book about the frustrations of ageing and life as his wife's carer in the not-so-fast lane of the Zzzzzzzzz Generation, and *The Twilight Escort Agency*, an hilarious and bawdy account of a mythical escort agency for the 'more mature' client, have enjoyed very positive independent reader response, as has his third novel, the whimsical comedy crime-fantasy, ideal for cat lovers, *Code Name: Millicent – The Cat Intelligence Agent Who Came Out of the Cold.*

The Tourist from the Light, an intriguing paranormal romance with an underlying theme of a thought-provoking alternative spiritual philosophy, followed. His fifth novel, *The Burning Boy*, is an exciting action/crime page-turner based on the horrors that haunt an ex-Vietnam War cameraman who returns to Australia in the mid seventies and becomes inadvertently involved in a sophisticated and lethal people-smuggling racket.

Bryon's beloved wife of 45 years, Marie, suffered a disastrous stroke in 2000 and he retired to become her full-time carer until she passed on in 2014. Bryon went on to write a memoir of his career and his married life, *A Light at the End*, which received numerous 5-star favourable reviews.

With the legalisation of gay marriage and acceptance of sexual equality, Bryon then changed course and wrote *Naked Warrior*, a gay, erotic love story based on Bryon's belief in Reincarnation.

Intrigued and inspired by an old friend's unresolved story of the tragic murder of her daughter in 1988, they collaborated to co-write *Not in the Public Interest*, published in 2019.